NOTHING SACRED

in the Halls of Ivy, to Max Shulman! . .
The great man wrote this famous lampoon
on campus life when he was a barefoot-
youth-with-cheek-of-brass, fresh out of the
University of Minnesota—and we mean *fresh!*

There is not a college institution, from how
to be employed as a star football player,
to free love, free verse, free beer, and
free-for-all scrimmages in sorority boudoirs,
which escapes the demon eye of America's
funniest writer.

Here is one of the most talked-about,
most hilarious and irreverent books
ever written—

BAREFOOT BOY WITH CHEEK

Books by Max Shulman

❧ Published by Bantam Books

MAX SHULMAN

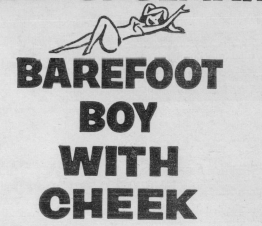

BAREFOOT
BOY
WITH
CHEEK

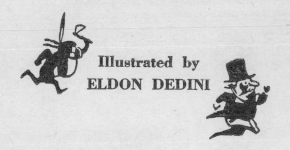

Illustrated by
ELDON DEDINI

Bantam Books

New York

BAREFOOT BOY WITH CHEEK

*A Bantam Book / published by arrangement with
Doubleday and Company, Inc.*

PRINTING HISTORY

*Doubleday edition published April 1943
2nd printing........April 1944
3rd printing ..... October 1944
Garden City edition published December 1944
2nd printing....November 1944
3rd printing......January 1945
4th printing........April 1945
5th printing ....May 1945
Bantam edition published January 1959*

*Bantam Books are published by Bantam Books, Inc. Its
trade-mark, consisting of the words "Bantam Books"
and the portrayal of a bantam, is registered in the
U. S. Patent Office and in other countries. Marca
Registrada. Printed in the United States of America.
Bantam Books, Inc., 25 West 45th St., New York 36, N. Y.*

NOTE

ALL CHARACTERS AND EVENTS in this book are fictitious. The University of Minnesota is, of course, wholly imaginary. I think it would be of some interest to the reader to know how I happened to pick the name "Minnesota."

It is a combination of two Indian words—"Minne" meaning a place where four spavined men and a minor woman ate underdone pemmican, and "sota" meaning the day the bison got away because the hunter's wife blunted his arrows in a fit of pique.

The combination of these two words means little, if anything, but the reader must consider that they are the only two Indian words I know.

—M. S.

CHAPTER I

THE MORNING of the big day dawned bright and clear. As the rosy fingers of the sun crept through my window and illuminated the C&H on my homemade bed sheet, I could scarcely contain myself. "Huzzah!" I shouted. "Huzzah!"

I bounded joyously from my bed. I bounded right back again. My drop-seat pajamas had become entangled in a bedspring during the night. Disengaging myself, I ran to wake Mother. "Mother," I called. "Mother, give me to eat."

But lovable old Mother had anticipated me. She had been up for hours. While I had lain in drowsyland, she had slaughtered the brood sow and bustled about preparing the morning meal. When I came into the kitchen, my favorite breakfast was already on the table.

"Mother!" I cried. "Johnson grass and brala suet. Just for me."

"Set down and eat, slugabed," she chided gently. "You don't want to be late the first day."

I could not help taking her in my arms and kissing her careworn cheek. A person can choose his friends and select a wife, but he has only one mother, I always say. The trouble with many of us is that we don't appreciate our mothers. I think that a certain day should be set aside each year and dedicated to mothers. It could be called "Mother's Day."

"Son," she said, "you ain't my baby no more."

"The hell you say, Mother," I said. "The hell you say."

1

"You're agoin' off to thet air university and get your haid all full of l'arnin', and you're gonna fergit your pore old igerant mother."

"Aw, you're not so dumb," I protested.

"Yes, I be," she declared. "I don't know no more than your old houn' dog Edmund layin' over there by the stove."

I jumped up from the table. "Now just you be careful what you're saying about Edmund. I don't mean to have that dog run down when I'm here. He's a mighty smart dog." I whistled to him. "Play dead, Edmund," I said. "See," I told Mother. "Look at how he obeys. All four feet sticking up in the air."

"He ain't playin', son," Mother said softly. "I didn't want to tell you. He's been dead since Friday."

Edmund dead! I couldn't believe it. Why, only last Friday I had seen him happily flushing grouse. In his excitement he had flushed too many, and we had had to call a plumber. But it was all fixed now, and Edmund was forgiven. Naturally, I had punished him, but—— No. No! I couldn't have——

"Mother!" I cried.

"Yes, son," she said. "He died right after. That last time you ran over him with the car did it."

I stumbled over to the window and pressed my hot forehead against the pane. A cloud passed over the sun, and it began to rain. The room was oppressively quiet. A loon cried over the lake.

Father came into the kitchen. "Good morning, son," he said. "I came to say good-by before you went off to the University."

"Thank you," I said simply.

"Button your fly," Mother said.

"Oh, button your lip," Father exclaimed testily, and hit her in the mouth with a skillet. Mother went to weld her dentures.

Father came over and put his arm around me. "Son, today you are entering a new phase of your life."

"Oh, can't you leave me alone?" I snapped. "Can't anybody leave me alone?"

Father drew back. "Why, son, what's the matter? This should be the happiest day in your life."

I laughed ironically. "The happiest day of your life, he says."

"No, no," Father interrupted. "I said the happiest day *in* your life. Not *of—in!*"

"Oh. Excuse me. The happiest day in your life, he says." I lifted my clenched fists. "Oh, ironical gods! What a mockery you have made of this day."

"Why, son, what——"

I pointed mutely to Edmund.

"I understand," said Father simply.

The door opened and two men from the animal rescue league came in. They took Edmund. "Neighbors been complaining," one of them explained.

Father put an arm around my shaking shoulders. "You know, son," he said, "I had a dog once. A little Pekingese bitch named Anna May."

"Is it true what they say about the Pekingese, Father?" I asked.

He winked obscenely and continued: "She wasn't much of a dog, I guess. She couldn't hunt. She was no good as a watchdog. All she did all day long was lie on a chaise longue reading slim yellow French novels and eating bonbons. But when I came home at night from a hard day at the egg candlery, Anna May was always waiting, wagging her little tail and being sick on the rug. I—I guess I loved her, that's all," Father said.

"I understand," I said simply.

"But I didn't have Anna May long. One day my cousin May Fuster came to visit me. You remember May, don't you, son?"

"Of course," I said. "Whatever became of her?"

"It's a long story. She ran off with a full-blooded Chippewa named Alf Mountainclimbing. He took her to La Paz, Bolivia, where he found employment as a clerk in an Adam hat store. At first May loved it down there. She used to watch the colorful *pesos* riding around in their old-fashioned *tortillas*. Every afternoon she used to lie down and take a *hacienda*. During the carnival season she would put on her *vincent lopez* and dance in the street with the rest of the happy natives. In her own words she was, as the expression goes, very *muy Usted*.

3

"But a cloud passed over the sunshine of her life. Alf's Chippewa heritage manifested itself. He started to drink heavily. One could always find him sprawled drunkenly over a table in one of the lower-class *cojones* of La Paz. He lost his position at the hat store. Poor May, in order to keep body and soul together, was forced into inter-American relations with the natives.

"Alf grew progressively worse. His alcoholic brain cells finally failed him. One day he dropped to all fours and declared that he was a pinball machine. From that day on he remained in that position, complaining occasionally that he was being tilted.

"May's sultry Northern beauty brought her a large and varied clientele. One of her patrons was Ed Frenesi, the local bullfight impresario. Frenesi remarked the supple grace of her limbs and suggested to her that she should become a female bullfighter.

"Of course she scoffed at the idea. But after he offered her 5,000 *muchachas* (about thirty-four hundred dollars) while she was learning and 5,000 more for every bull she killed, May accepted."

"I understand," I said simply.

"Then began a rigorous training period. First she trained with less dangerous bulls from which the horns had been removed. May was up early every morning making passes at the dehorns. All day long she practiced in the hot sun with a draped cape and a gored sword. She retired every evening at eight, and after reading Hemingway for an hour fell into the deep sleep of fatigue.

"Frenesi watched her progress with considerable satisfaction. He saw how easily she mastered the intricate art of dominating the bull, and he knew that if everything went right he would have a great attraction. He taught May by easy stages until she learned the ultimate accomplishment in the bullfighter's craft—the Veronica, or killing a bull while your hair hangs over one eye. Then Frenesi knew that she was ready for her debut. He Latinized her name to Yanqui Imperialismo, and splashed posters all over La Paz.

"Frenesi's shrewd showmanship had its desired effect. For weeks before the bullfight nobody in La Paz talked about anything but *el toreador broad*—the lady bullfighter. From all the surrounding territories people poured into La Paz. Hotel rooms were filled almost immediately, and thousands of visitors had to sleep on makeshift *frijoles* in the lobbies. The wineshops and cafés were unable to handle all their trade. Alf, May's husband, took in a considerable sum posing as a pinball machine in a downtown tavern. La Paz's choked streets resounded with good-natured cries of 'I spit in the milk of your motor,' and 'I this and that on your this.' The land office did a land-office business."

Father took a guitar from the mantel and struck chords as he continued his narrative. "The day of the big fight dawned bright and clear. In the morning Frenesi went down to the bull pen and selected a crowd pleaser named Harry Holstein as May's opponent. May went to her dressing room at the arena where her cross-eyed seamstress named Pilar helped her with the involved business of dressing. May was nervous and frightened, but Pilar reassured her. 'Do not be afraid, my little,' she said. 'We all got to go sometime.'

"At last May heard the fanfare, and she knew that the *Presidente* had entered his box. The fight was about to begin. Suddenly May was in the center of the hot white sand of the arena. A roar rose from a hundred thousand throats. A gate swung open, and Harry Holstein, pawing and snorting, charged into the ring.

"Now the fear left May. Coolly she prepared to nimbly sidestep the initial charge of the beast. But, alas, her cross-eyed seamstress had tied the laces of her two shoes together. She could not move.

"May was impaled on the horns of the bull. What a dilemma! The attendants rushed from the sidelines to rescue her. The angry, cheated people in the stands cut off their ears and threw them into the arena with enraged cries of '*Olé! Olé!*'

"May eventually recovered. As soon as she could, she left La Paz. Her name was anathema in the town. She tried to see Frenesi once, but he instructed his housekeeper to pour hot water on her.

"So she wandered from one South American city to

another, eking out a bare living tuning guitars and dealing double Canfield. Today, a broken woman, she earns a meager subsistence as a harbor buoy in Havana."

"But what about your Pekingese, Father?" I asked.

"Gad, son, look at the time!" Father exclaimed. "You'll be late for school."

"Gracious!" I cried. "It is late. And I want to see somebody before I go off to the University."

"It couldn't be Lodestone La Toole, could it?" asked Father slyly.

I blushed becomingly.

"Good-by, Father," I called, and closed the door on his kindly chuckling.

CHAPTER II

Le crayon est sur la table.—VOLTAIRE

AS I MADE MY WAY up the devious path that led to the grassy knoll where I knew Lodestone would be waiting, my heart was heavy with the thought of leaving her. And when I achieved a promontory and saw her in the middle distance, her lithe young legs stretched before her, the sun casting golden ripples on her tawny hair, I knew it would be hard, hard, hard.

I hastened to her with love-quickened steps. Then I was beside her, and my funny little crooked smile gleamed across my bronzed face, and my brooding gray eyes crinkled at the corners. "Lodestone," I said simply.

"Asa," she breathed, for that was my name.

She was in my arms. Our lips met. Time crashed wildly about us as the entire universe was resolved into our embrace. I was laved in the fragrance of her. I knew a pulsing, mounting ecstasy. Then suddenly I was still, at peace in a pastel world.

"I'm hungry," said Lodestone at length. "Can't we get something to eat?"

"Not now, my own. I haven't time. I must leave you in oh, too short a time to go to the University of Minnesota."

"Maybe we could just get a hamburger. That don't take long."

"I am going," I continued, "and yet I am not going. For you will always be with me. Wherever I am, whatever I do, I shall always think of you."

"There's a White Castle down the road a piece. They have real nice hamburgers. It don't take them hardly no time to fix them neither."

7

"Who can say that we are apart when we are together in our hearts? Is there, indeed, a closer proximity than the spiritual?"

"We could get a little pot of beans too. They got the beans already made. All they have to do is put them in a little pot."

"Lodestone—oh, I know this will sound crazy, but believe me anything is possible for two in love—every night at midnight, no matter where I am or what I am doing, I will pause for a moment and think of you. You do the same, and I know we will both be able to feel that we are together. Promise me you will, Lodestone."

I took her two hands in mine and gazed into her green-flecked golden eyes. My mouth found the garden of her lips. I was engulfed in the yielding delight of her. And then the earth was quiet, save for the song of a full-throated bobolink.

"Listen to the bird, Lodestone," I whispered.

"Birds. Next month the pheasant season opens. Pa's gonna shoot us some pheasants. Yum, yum." She rubbed her tummy expressively.

"That bird song is our love, Lodestone—free and gay and young."

"I like quail, too, but sometimes they're kinda gamy. I like pheasants the best."

"We will grow old, you and I, Lodestone, but our love will be young always, forever and ever." I sang softly, "When your hair has turned to silver . . ."

"When your hair has turned to silver," she mused. "They played that there at Ma and Pa's silver wedding anniversary. What a party that was. We had a whole shoat with an apple in his mouth barbecued on a spit. I eat till I thought I'd bust. My aunt Alice B. Toklas, she eat so much she got bloated, and they had to roll her home. Talk about eat."

"I'm going to leave you, Lodestone. I'm going off to the University. It isn't for myself I'm going. A man can always get along. It's just that I want to be worthy of you, my adored one. I want to make something of myself for your sake. I want to deserve you, and I want you to be proud of me."

8

I laid my cheek in the classic curve of her throat. My lips sought the cool alabaster of her skin. Then I was swept aloft on the pounding crescendo of our united psyches. Now all was tranquil, and the scent of clover filled my passive nostrils.

I turned my eyes, dark with tenderness, upon her. "Often I wake in the middle of the night and cry out, 'Tear mine tongue from out mine head, tear mine eyes from out mine sockets, but tear me not from Lodestone!' And then a voice deep down inside me says, 'Fond child, you must go for her sake. She would have it so.'"

"Ma always puts a bowl of lard drippings and one hundred and twenty slices of bread on the table, and then tells us to go ahead and eat. Ma never was one to stint. Like she says, what's food for if not to eat it? Lord, how we eat."

"Even now I can feel the thrill that will come when we two meet again. Absence makes the heart grow fonder may be just an old saying and a bromo, but all the same, it's true, true—as true, Lodestone, as my love for you."

"Will I ever forget the time Pa slaughtered the milch cow? She was a old cow. The last time Pa took her over to Lafe Sorenson's bull to have her serviced, the bull just turned her down flat. So Pa slaughtered her. I just eat and eat and eat till I like to have died."

"Time is short, Lodestone, and I must not waste it groping for words to express my love for you. Mine is not the poet's tongue. Not yet. Perhaps when I come back from the University I shall be able to express myself more adequately. Someday—ah, but it is but a dream—someday perhaps I shall be a writer. But I must not even let myself think of that now. And so, Lodestone, this is it—not good-by, but *au Wiedersehen.*"

I held her close against me, drinking in the perfume of her hair. I was transported in the familiar, unknown rapture of her. All creation shimmered transfixed in the evanescent exaltation of now. Then, like a leaf, I was wafted to rest.

"Jesus," she said, "can't we get something to eat?"

"I guess I could use a couple of eggs," I confessed.

Hand in hand we floated down from the grassy knoll.

CHAPTER III

Ou est mon chapeau?—ANATOLE FRANCE

ST. PAUL AND MINNEAPOLIS extend from the Mississippi River like the legs on a pair of trousers. Where they join is the University of Minnesota.

I stood that day and gazed at the campus, my childish face looking up, holding wonder like a cup; my little feet beating time, time, time, in a sort of runic rhyme. A fraternity man's convertible ran me down, disturbing my reverie. "Just a flesh wound," I mumbled to disinterested passersby.

With eager steps I proceeded to explore the campus. All around me was the hum of happy men at work. Here were masons aging a building so they could hang ivy on it. There were chiselers completing the statue of Cyrus Thresher, first regent of the University. It was Thresher, as you know, who said, "It takes a heap o' learnin' to make a school a school." Yonder were landscapers cleverly trimming a twelve-foot hedge to spell "Minnesota, Minnesota, rah, rah, ree. Little brown jug, how we love thee."

The architecture at Minnesota is very distinctive, and thereby hangs a tale. It goes back a good many years, back to the time when the mighty, sprawling University was just an infant. At that time Art Chaff, the son of a wealthy Minneapolis flour miller named Elihu Chaff, was expelled from Harvard for playing buck euchre on the Sabbath. Old Elihu was deeply incensed by the indignity. He was determined that Art should go to college, and, moreover, to a bigger college than Harvard.

11

So Elihu went to work on the University of Minnesota campus. He erected twenty buildings. They all looked like grain elevators, for that is what Elihu intended to use them for after Art had been graduated. But Elihu never fulfilled his plan.

One week end Elihu went fishing, accompanied only by an Indian guide named Ralph Duckhonking. They went into a deep forest, and after two days Duckhonking came out alone. He was wearing Elihu's suit and carrying all of his valuables. He said he knew nothing about Elihu's disappearance. Duckhonking was indicted for murder, but he was never tried because it was impossible to obtain twelve English-speaking veniremen in that judicial district. Duckhonking walked about free until he died more than twenty years later of nepotism. This case later became famous as the *Crédit Mobilier* scandal.

Elihu's elevators, therefore, remained part of the University. In fact, out of respect to Elihu, all the buildings which were subsequently erected on the campus were built to resemble grain elevators.

But this was no time to be gawking about the campus. I had things to do. First I had to see Mr. Ingelbretsvold, my freshman adviser, about making out a program of studies for the year. Obtaining directions from a friendly upperclassman who sold me a freshman button, freshman cap, subscription to *Ski-U-Mah,* the campus honor magazine, a map of the campus, and a souvenir score card of last year's home-coming game, I proceeded to the office of Mr. Ingelbretsvold.

A line of freshmen stood in front of his door. I knew how they must feel, about to embark on this great adventure, and I could not help cheerily hollering "Halloa" to them. They stoned me in an amiable fashion.

At last a voice came from behind the door bidding me come in. How my heart beat as I opened the door and trod across the luxuriant burlap rug to Mr. Ingelbretsvold's desk.

"My name is Asa Hearthrug and I've come for advice," I said.

He stood up and smiled at me kindlily. "Sit down, young man," he said.

"Thank you," I said, making a low curtsey.

"Well, it's certainly a nice day."

"Yes," I agreed. "Almost twelve inches of rain since sunup."

"That's what I meant," he said. "It's a nice rain. It will help the potato crop."

"Yes," I agreed, "it should wash out every potato in Minnesota."

"That's what I meant," he said. "It will get rid of those damn potatoes. People are eating altogether too many potatoes. But enough of this meteorological chitchat. Let's get down to business. First of all, I want you to know that I'm your friend."

I licked his hand gratefully.

"You are about to enter a new phase of your life. I wonder whether you realize just how important this is."

"Oh, I do, sir, I do," I exclaimed.

"Shut up when I'm talking," he said. "Now, I have a little story that I like to tell to freshmen to impress them with the importance of college. I have had a great many students who were graduated from Minnesota and went out to take their places in the world come back after many years and say to me, 'Mr. Ingelbretsvold, I can never thank you enough for that little story you told me when I first came to the University.' Yes, young man, this story has helped a great many people, and I hope it will help you."

"So tell it already," I said.

"Well, sir, when I was a boy I had a good friend named Kyrie Eleison. We went through grade school and high school together, and on the night we were graduated from high school I said to him, 'Well, Kyrie, what are you going to do now?'

" 'Oh,' he said, 'I've got a chance to get a job in a nepotism business in North Dakota.'

" 'Kyrie,' I told him, 'don't take it. Come to college with me, or else you'll always regret it.'

"But he didn't choose to take my advice. I went to college, and he took the job. Yes, he did well at his work. By the time he was thirty he had seventy-five million dollars, and he has been getting richer ever since.

He built a fine big house in which he holds the most lavish social affairs in the whole Northwest.

"Well, sir, one night I was invited to a party at Kyrie's house. I rented a suit and went. The house was filled with prominent people. A hundred-and-twenty-piece orchestra was playing. When we went in for dinner the table groaned with all sorts of expensive delicacies. And at the head of the table sat Kyrie, the monarch of all he surveyed.

"But during the course of the dinner a well-dressed young woman leaned over and said to Kyrie, 'Who was the eighth avatar of Vishnu?' and Kyrie, for all his wealth and power, did not know the answer."

"How ghastly!" I cried, throwing up my hands.

"Yes," said Mr. Ingelbretsvold. "You will find that sort of thing all through life. People come up to you on the street and say, 'Does a paramecium beat its flagella?' or 'How many wheels has a fiacre?' or 'When does an oryx mate?' and if you have not been to college, you simply cannot answer them."

"But that cannot happen to me. I am going to the University," I said.

"Ah, but it can," Mr. Ingelbretsvold answered. "It happens to many who go to college."

"But how?"

"You see, my boy, a great many people go to college to learn how to *do* something. They study medicine or law or engineering, and when they are through they know how to trepan a skull or where to get a writ of estoppel or how to find the torque of a radial engine. But just come up to them and ask how many caliphs succeeded Mohammed or who wrote *Baby Duncan's Whistling Lung* and they stare at you blankly."

I shuddered. "Oh, please, Mr. Ingelbretsvold," I begged, "what must I do?"

"You must do like I tell you. You must let college make you a well-rounded-out personality. That is the chief function and purpose of this University: to make you a well-rounded-out personality. Now you get out a pencil and paper and write down the names of the courses

I am going to give you. If you follow this program you will find yourself a well-rounded-out personality."

I took out a pencil and poised it over my dickey bosom.

"Ready. Here they are: Races and Cultures of Arabia, Egypt, and North Africa; Ethnology of India; History of Architecture; Greek; Latin; Sixteenth-Century Literature; Seventeenth-Century Literature; Eighteenth-Century Litterature; Nineteenth-Century Literature; Twentieth-Century Literature; Geography; Ancient History; Medieval History; Modern History; Ancient Philosophy; Modern Philosophy; Contemporary Philosophy; History of Religion; American Government; British Government; Chinese Government; Japanese Government; Lett Government; First Aid; Public Health; General Psychology; Psychology of Learning; Psychology of Advertising; Psychology of Literature; Psychology of Art; Psychology of Behavior; Animal Psychology; Abnormal Psychology; Norwegian; Swedish; Danish; French; German; Russian; Italian; Lett; Urban Sociology; Rural Sociology; Juvenile Sociology; Statistical Sociology; Criminology; Penology, Elocution; Speech Pathology; and Canoe Paddling.

"That will do for a start. As you go into these courses you will find others that will interest you too."

"And these will make me a well-rounded-out personality?" I asked.

He laughed gently. "Oh no, my boy. That is only a small but essential part of rounding out your personality. There is the social life too." He nudged me and winked. "A fellow can have a good time here."

"Sir," I said, and blushed.

"But you'll soon find out all about that. Now, one more thing. In addition to the work you do for these courses I have named you should do a lot of reading that has not been assigned in your classes. Do you read anything now?"

"A mystery story now and then," I confessed.

"Oh, have you read Rex Snout's latest, *The Case of the Gelded Gnu?*"

"No, but I read the one before that, *The Case of the Missing Lynx.*"

"I missed that one. What was it about?"

"Well, a horribly mutilated corpse is found on the railroad tracks near Buffalo. This corpse is in such a state that it is impossible to identify it or even to tell whether it is a man or a woman. The story is concerned almost entirely with trying to establish the identity of the corpse. In the end it is discovered that it is not a corpse at all, but a pan of waffle batter that fell out of the window of a New York Central dining car."

"How interesting. Well, I guess that's all the time I can give you. Others are waiting," he said, taking cognizance of the stones they were throwing through the window.

"Just one more thing, Mr. Ingelbretsvold," I said. "I don't know quite how to say this, but I think I would like to be a writer when I grow up. Will the program you made out for me help me to be a writer?"

"Why, bless you, child," Mr. Ingelsbretsvold said, "you follow that program and there's nothing else you can be."

CHAPTER IV

Pommes de terre sont bon.—MOLIÈRE

THE UNIVERSITY OF MINNESOTA builds not only minds; it also builds bodies. Before you can enter the University you must undergo a thorough and rigorous examination at the Student Health Service. Minnesota has one of the finest health services in the country. Here prominent doctors, serving without compensation, give unstintingly of their time and wisdom that youth of Minnesota might be strong.

I shall always remember, with a mixture of gratitude and admiration, the day I went through the Health Service for my examination. I was extensively examined by not one, but many doctors, each an expert in his particular branch of medicine.

First I was sent to the bone surgeon. He was sitting at his desk reading a copy of *Film Fun.* "How many arms and legs you got?" he asked, without putting down the *Film Fun.*

"Two," I answered.

"Two altogether?"

"No sir, two of each."

"O.K. You're all right. Go ahead," he said, still looking at the *Film Fun.*

I proceeded to the office of the heart doctors. Because heart examination is a delicate, involved process, two doctors are assigned to that duty. When I came into the office, they were standing by the window dropping paper bags filled with water on pedestrians.

"I had an interesting case the other day," said one

to the other. "I was listening to a kid's heart and it was the damnedest thing I ever heard. It didn't thump. It chimed in three notes."

"What do you know?" said the second. "What caused that?"

"I couldn't find out for a long time," answered the first. "It wasn't until I went way back into the kid's history that I found the solution. His mother was frightened by an NBC station break."

"Well, what do you know?" said the second. "Say, I heard of another interesting case yesterday. Dr. Curette in plastic surgery told me about it. A man came in to see him. The fellow didn't have a nose."

"No nose?" said the first. "How did he smell?"

"Terrible," said the second.

"Oh, Harold," said the first, "you're more fun than a barrel of monkeys."

I cleared my throat. They turned and noticed me for the first time.

"I've come for a heart examination," I said.

"You look all right. Go ahead," they said.

They went over to the sink to fill some more bags with water.

My next stop was the weighing room. I stepped on the scale, my weight was recorded, and a doctor said, "You make friends easily. You are a good worker although you are a little inclined to put things off. You are going to make a long trip on water."

I gave him a penny and proceeded to the abdominal clinic. The doctor was sitting at a table building a boat in a bottle. "Ever have to get up in the middle of the night?" he asked.

"Yes sir," I answered.

"Hmm," he said. "I'm going to have a little trouble with the mizzenmast. Know anything about boats?"

"Some," I confessed modestly.

"I love boats," he said. "I love the sea. Right now I'd love to be on a trim little schooner hauling a cargo of oscars from the levant. I love the good feel of a stout ship on a rough sea. Perhaps a nor'wester would blow up, and all the hearty mates would be on the deck

pulling together while the grizzled old skipper stood on the bridge and yelled his orders: 'Keelhaul the bosun! Jettison the supercargo!' "

"My, you certainly know a lot about boats," I said admiringly.

He lowered his eyes. "I should. I was cuckold on the Yale crew in 1912. But enough of this. So you have to get up in the middle of the night?"

"Yes sir. You see, my sister Morningstar keeps company with an engineer on the Natchez, Mobile, and Duluth railroad. About a year ago he got put on a night run, and Morningstar never used to get to see him. She complained so much that he finally had a sidetrack built into our back yard.

"Now when he comes by at night he runs the train into our back yard for a while. I have to get up in the middle of the night and go out and keep his steam up while he comes in the house and trifles with Morningstar."

But he wasn't listening. He was fiddling with his boat in the bottle. "Wonder which side is starboard," he mumbled.

I left quietly for the chiropodist's office.

The doctor was sitting behind his desk playing "Your Feets Too Big" on a jew's-harp when I came in.

"How did you get here?" he asked.

"Why, I walked."

"Well, then," he said. "your feet are all right. You're lucky. There was a girl in here the other day whose feet were in terrible shape. She had been wearing such high heels that she constantly leaned forward at a forty-five-degree angle. Gave the impression of being on a ski slide."

"What did you do for her?" I asked.

"Cut off her legs, naturally. She's much happier now. She's made a lot of new friends who affectionately call her 'Shorty.' "

I made as if to go.

"Wait a minute. Know how I got interested in chiropody?"

"No sir," I said, for I did not.

He giggled. "I got webbed feet, that's why." He leaped

up from his chair and ran around the room quacking wildly. Water was rolling off his back.

Now I went to the last office, the psychiatrist's. He was driving golf balls through the window. An angry crowd was collecting outside. "Any insanity in your family?" he asked.

"Oh, not really insanity," I said. "Maybe some of them act a little funny sometimes, but I wouldn't call it insanity. Uncle Bert, for instance, he's in Washington now circulating a petition to free Sacco and Vanzetti.

"And Cousin Roger. He's got a little farm near Des Moines. Every day he hauls his produce to Des Moines in a square-wheeled cart.

"And Uncle Donald. He started a million-dollar suit against the Reynolds Tobacco Company last year. He says he got a hump on his back from smoking Camels.

"And Aunt Yetta. Every time she needs a little money, she pulls out a tooth and puts it under her pillow.

"And then there's Cousin Booker, who thinks he's got a diamond in his navel, and Aunt Melanie who burns churches, and Uncle Alex who hangs on the wall and says he's a telephone, and Uncle Milton who has been standing in a posthole since 1924.

"But I wouldn't call that insanity exactly, would you, Doctor?"

"Oh, certainly not," he said. "They're probably just a little tired. Well, my boy, the examination is all over. Let me congratulate you. You are now a student at the University of Minnesota."

Tears filled my eyes and my throat was all choked up.

"Don't try to talk," said the doctor. "Just hold me tight. I want to remember you always, just like this."

In a little while I was all right, and I left, hoping with all my heart that I would prove worthy of the consideration that my new alma mater had lavished upon me.

CHAPTER V

Qui est dans le corridor?—SAINT-SAENS

AFTER I LEFT the Health Service I went for a walk. I wanted to think about all the wonderful things that had happened to me. I could scarcely believe that in just a few days I was going to walk into a university class, a belonger, a cog in a great machine where everyone puts his nose to the grindstone and pulls together. I glowed all over as I walked upon the handsome promenade called fraternity row.

Minnesota has one of the finest fraternity rows in the country. Behind luxuriant, well-kept lawns stand the ornate but tasteful fronts of the fraternity houses. Doric columns adorn their façades, and through the leaded panes of their windows I could see gay, well-dressed young men lounging casually in the living rooms. My fellow students, I thought rapturously. I gave a little jump in my unbridled joy. As I landed, two cunningly hinged sidewalk stones gave way, and I hurtled into a pit below.

"We got one," someone yelled. Immediately two youths beset me and tied me with baling wire. Then I was carried through a devious tunnel into the living room of a fraternity house. "We got one, Roger," announced the bearers.

The one called Roger was sitting at a table playing Michigan rummy with three others. "O.K.," he said. The others drew guns, and each one walked over to a door. "Untie him," Roger commanded.

The two who had brought me in produced an acetylene torch and loosed me. Roger pulled out a buffer and dental

22

floss and got his teeth ready. Then he smiled. "I'm Roger Hailfellow, the president. I'm certainly glad that you decided on this fraternity. Yes sir, you can't find a better fraternity than Alpha Cholera. How about that, fellows?" he asked, turning to the three who were guarding the exits.

"Friend, you did right," they said to me.

"I'll tell you, chum," said Roger, putting his arm around me, sticking a cigarette in my mouth, and lighting it, "there's fraternities and there's fraternities. I don't like to knock anybody, but there's some bad fraternities as well as good fraternities. A fellow who joins a bad fraternity is almost as bad off as a fellow who don't join no fraternity at all. And you know how bad off a fellow is who don't join no fraternity at all. Damn barb." Roger spat angrily.

The three at the doors fired shots into the wall to indicate their feelings about a fellow who didn't join any fraternity.

"But you're lucky," Roger continued, sticking another cigarette in my mouth and lighting it. "You picked the best fraternity first crack off the bat. How about that, fellows?"

"Friend, you did right," they said.

"Yes sir, the very best. Alpha Cholera isn't one of those little upstart fraternities. No sir. Do you know when we were founded?"

"No," I said.

"Five hundred B.C. Alpha Cholera was founded in ancient Greece by three fellows named Aeschylus, Sophocles, and Euripides. They did not give their last names. Even in those days people knew a good thing when they saw one, and all the right people in Greece joined Alpha Cholera. The spring formal at the Parthenon was the high spot of the social year in Athens. They had the best orchestra in the country, Oedipus Rex. 'Fling and flex with Oedipus Rex' was his slogan.

"But just like it is today, Alpha Cholera was choosy about who it let in. The mayor of Athens, Nick, tried to get his son into the fraternity, but Alpha Cholera was not going to take nobody with a ram's head. It meant banishment.

"So the members hied themselves off to Rome. They were carried most of the way on the back of their sergeant at arms, a chap named Aeneas. When they finally reached Rome, they were so exhausted that they collapsed on the ground. They would have perished, had it not been for a passing she-wolf who suckled them.

"In Rome Alpha Cholera did not fare well. The members were relentlessly hunted out and murdered by the barbarous Romans. Finally there was only one Alpha Cholera left, a fellow called Androcles. He hid for a time in the basement of a sympathetic Roman candlestick maker named Phelps or Mazinik. Eventually Androcles was apprehended, and it was decided that he was to be thrown to the lions.

"While thousands of spectators sat in the Colosseum and roared for blood, Androcles bravely entered the lion's cage. The beast rushed at him. Stout-hearted Androcles proceeded to grapple. Unwittingly, as he seized the lion's paw, he gave him the secret Alpha Cholera handshake. The lion paused. He licked Androcles' face and refused to do further battle. He, too, was an Alpha Cholera, Swahili chapter.

"Androcles was spared and lived to carry forward the torch of Alpha Cholera. After his death, we know that Alpha Cholera continued to exist, but we are not sure of the details. We believe that there was a chapter in Pompeii. When the noted archaeologist, Dudley Digs, excavated the ruins of Pompeii, he found a corpse wearing a pin that bore the initials A.C. We think that stood for Alpha Cholera. Digs, himself, holds to another theory. The corpse who was wearing the pin also held a dulcimer in his hand, and Digs believes that the A.C. meant "Ad Carthage" where the Roman musicians' union was going to hold its convention the year of the Pompeiian disaster.

"Be that as it may, we know that somehow Alpha Cholera went forward unbrokenly. In the writings of Cellini we find this passage: 'I saw this night a comely wench upon the thoroughfare. After pleasant amenities she accompanied me to my quarters where we deported ourselves pleasantly until she, seeing a bauble upon my blouse, expressed a desire for it. I gave her that and other things

FLING
AND
FLEX
WITH
OediPus
Rex

and having done, hit her in the mouth, took back the bauble, and flung her from my casement.' The bauble was, of course, an Alpha Cholera pin.

"We are certain, too, that Robespierre was an Alpha Cholera. The motto for the French Revolution was originally 'Liberty, Equality.' Robespierre inserted the 'Fraternity.'

"And who do you think brought Alpha Cholera to America? The pilgrim fathers, no less. They were an Alpha Cholera chapter in London, but they lost the lease on their house when their landlady, the old lady of Threadneedle Street, found out that they were dancing on Saturday nights. She hated dancing since years before when she had gone out with an adagio dancer named Ike, who had snatched her purse and thrown her into a passing circus wagon where she had been assaulted four times by an orang-utan. So the pilgrim fathers came to America where nobody could interfere with their Saturday-night hops."

"My. You certainly have an illustrious history," I exclaimed, removing the cigarettes from my mouth so I could talk.

"Friend, you said right," said the three at the doors.

"Now, you just sit here and smoke a cigarette while I get you a pledge card to sign," Roger said, inserting another cigarette in my mouth.

"Well, wait a minute," I protested. "I really hadn't intended to join a fraternity today. I was just walking along the sidewalk here when I happened to fall into your pit. I really wasn't thinking about joining a fraternity. I hope you understand I have nothing against your fraternity. It seems to be a totally admirable institution. And I certainly do appreciate all these cigarettes I am smoking. I am grateful, too, for the time you have spent telling me all about Alpha Cholera. But, to be perfectly frank, I wasn't even thinking about joining a fraternity—at least, not today."

The three with guns moved in on me. Roger waved them back. "Of course," he said simply. "How stupid of me. You want a little time to think it over. Well, why don't you have lunch here, and perhaps we can talk about it some more?"

"Oh, I don't think I should. You have done too much for me already."

"Oh, pooh," said Roger. "It's nothing. Harry, go get something to eat for our friend."

One of the doorkeepers left.

"Really, Roger," I cried, "you shouldn't!"

"Tut, tut," Roger said. "I want you to think of the Alpha Cholera house as your home away from home."

I felt a lump rise in my throat. "I think that's the nicest thing anybody has ever said to me," I said simply.

Roger lowered his eyes modestly. Harry came in with my lunch. I looked, and for a moment I thought my senses were deceiving me, for Harry had laid a plate of hominy grits before me, and they were arranged to spell out:

> *Alpha Cholera is glad you're here.*
> *Eat these grits in all good cheer.*

Unable to speak, I looked at Roger. He smiled reassuringly and bade me eat. As I started to eat, the three at the doors came over to Roger. They all patted me on the shoulder, and then, putting their arms about one another, proceeded to sing this song:

> *"Stand, good men, take off your hat*
> *To Alpha Cholera, our swell frat.*
> *In our midst you'll find no rat,*
> *And don't let anyone tell you that.*

> *"Be you lean or be you fat,*
> *Join Alpha Cholera, our swell frat.*
> *Since long ago, when first we mat,*
> *Our swell bunch is together yat."*

As their last soft chords died, I could see through the leaded panes of the window the flaming orb of the sun expire gently into the west. The earth was bathed in the soft pastel of the vanishing day.

"Want some salt on those grits?" Roger asked gently.

I shook my head, for my tears were salt enough. Understanding, Roger perceived my condition and said, "Let's go, fellows. He wants to be alone for a while." They patted my throbbing shoulders and left, still singing the Alpha Cholera song in close harmony.

I finished the grits and licked the plate so they wouldn't have to wash it. Then I wiped my nose on my sleeve and let my thoughts take possession of me. If somebody had told me before I came to the University that my fellow students were going to make such a to-do over me, I would have cried, "Go to, sirrah, and make not light of my innocence." But it was all true. Here was I, a complete stranger, taken without question into the bosom of my fellows. Ah, alma mater, you are indeed my adopted mother, I thought.

Roger and the others returned. "How was it?" Roger asked.

"The lunch? It was divine."

"Well, that gives you a rough idea of the kind of cuisine we have at Alpha Cholera. And hominy grits is only an example of what you'll get. We often have peanut-butter sandwiches, baked beans, turnip greens, and head cheese. And on legal holidays we always have mackerel."

"No!" I exclaimed.

"Yes," said Roger. "And would you believe it, our kitchen shows a profit year after year. But enough. Let's get down to business. Are you ready to join?"

The three at the doors had put their guns in their holsters. Now they drew them again.

"Well," I said, "how much does it cost?"

"Why, bless you," Roger said, "don't you worry about that. Come with me. I'll introduce you to some of the fellows."

He took me by the hand and led be upstairs to the dormitory. "We have one of the biggest B.M.O.C.'s in Alpha Cholera," he said, as we walked up the stairs.

"What's a B.M.O.C.?" I asked.

"A Big Man on Campus," he explained.

We stopped in front of a room near the head of the

stairs. "This room belongs to Eino Fflliikkiinncnn," Roger said reverently.

"Not Eino Fflliikkiinnenn, the football player!" I cried.

"Yes," said Roger. "He will be your fraternity brother."

I was all shaky inside as we entered Fflliikkiinnenn's room. He was standing in a corner beating his head methodically against the wall. "He's toughening up for the football season," Roger whispered.

"Eino," Roger called, "here's a man who wants to mcct you. He is going to pledge Alpha Cholera."

Eino grabbed my hand in a hearty grip. "Ay tink dot's real nice," he said. "Ay am happy to call you my brudder."

I did not trust myself to speak.

"Did I do good, Roger?" said Eino.

"Yes, Eino," Roger answered. "Now let go of his hand and go back to your exercises."

"Say, Roger," Eino said, "you didn't pay me yat dis mont'."

"Is that so?" said Roger. "Well, it's just an oversight. I'll see that you get your money right away."

"You batter," Eino said. "Ay got a goot offer from Mu Beta Fistula to live over dere. Dey pay on time too."

"I'll see that you get your money. Don't worry," said Roger.

"You batter," Eino said, "and cash. No more beer chips."

We left.

"Just think of bcing a fraternity brother of Eino Fflliikkiinnenn's," Roger said to me.

"I can't imagine anything more heavenly," I answered.

Roger rubbed his hands. "Well, then, should I get the pledge card?"

"Well, I don't know. I really wasn't thinking of joining a fraternity. I just happened to be walking by when I fell into——"

"Let's go take a look at our record collection," Roger interrupted.

We went downstairs to a large radio phonograph with an enclosed record cabinet. "We got everything," Roger said, "Goodman, Shaw, Basie, Dorsey, Herman, anything you want. All the new stuff too. Just got a new Andrews sisters disc today. 'Death and Transfiguration' on one side, 'Dope Me, Doctor, with a Sulfa Drug' on the other. Or maybe you like the heavier stuff. Symphonic. We got all you want. 'Filigree on Derriere's Variation of a Theme of Merde' recorded by the Rush City Four. And 'Afternoon of a Prawn.' Anything you want."

But again he was taking me somewhere. I followed him into a room piled waist high with pictures of girls. "Pictures here of every girl on the campus. Name, address, age, height, weight, habits, and food and liquor capacity written on the back. Also achievement records of all the fellows who have ever taken her out. Join Alpha Cholera and be sure what you're getting into."

"Land sakes," I said admiringly.

"Now will you pledge?" Roger asked.

I took his two hands in mine and looked him in the eyes. "Whatever you think best, Roger," I said simply.

He rubbed his hands rapidly, starting a minor conflagration on his cuffs. "Now, I suppose you want to discuss finances. Well, just you don't worry about that at all. I'll call our treasurer, and we'll have every little thing all straightened out as fast as you can say Jack Robinson. You'll like our treasurer."

Roger left and came back in a few minutes with the treasurer. "This is our treasurer, Shylock Fiscal," he said.

"Well, you finally got one," he said to Roger.

Roger smiled modestly.

"I was about to go to work," Shylock said.

"Where there's life there's hope," Roger reminded him.

"I just about gave up," Shylock confessed. "It's getting worse each year, what with the other houses serving meat and keeping a dozen B.M.O.C.'s and———"

"That reminds me," Roger interrupted. "Eino wants to get paid."

"Give him some beer chips," suggested Shylock.

"No, he wants cash."

"Cash, huh? Well, let's see what we can get from this turnip." Shylock turned to me. "I'm Shylock Fiscal," he said cheerily. "Just call me Shy. Everybody does. I guess it's because I'm not. Heh, heh, heh."

"Heh, heh, heh," laughed Roger.

I joined the general merriment. How good it was to share a good joke with good men.

"So you've decided to join Alpha Cholera?" Shylock continued. "Friend, you did right. You'll never regret it. There's nothing like a good fraternity, and Alpha Cholera is the best, isn't it, Roger?"

"Yes," Roger admitted.

"Yes sir. You can't beat a good fraternity. Good fellows living together in a good house, sharing each other's problems, making contacts that are going to be their most precious possessions in later life. But I don't have to tell you about the advantages. Anyone looking at you can tell that you know what the score is."

I blushed becomingly.

Shylock leaned closer and put his hand on my knee. "The surprising thing," he said, "is how reasonable Alpha Cholera is. I mean, looking at it intelligently. You and I know that in this world you don't get something for nothing; the best thing you can hope for is to get a lot of a little. And that's what you get when you join Alpha Cholera.

"Take dues, for instance. We charge $100 a month. I'll admit that $100 is a tidy sum. But remember, if you were going to take a suite in a hotel downtown while you went to school you'd pay a lot more. And besides, you'd be living alone. You wouldn't have all these swell kids to live with and share your problems. Furthermore, $100 a month dues keeps out the riffraff. You can be sure that you're living with the best people at Alpha Cholera.

"Now then, there's meals. Breakfast—$1.75. Lunch—$2.50. Dinner—$4.00. Now you know as well as I do that you can't pay too much for a good meal, attractively served in pleasant suroundings. How about that, Roger?"

"Yes," said Roger.

"And laundry. You just throw your dirty clothes down the chute, and the next time you see them, they're spick-and-span, all ready to wear. None of that wet-wash stuff here. No sir. And all for $12.50 a week.

"Then there's national dues; Alpha Cholera isn't one of your dinky one-chapter houses. Not on your life. You'll find an Alpha Cholera house on every major campus in the country. And that's important. Whenever you visit another college, you don't have to pay four or five dollars a night for a hotel room. You just go to the Alpha Cholera house and they'll put you up without charging you a cent. National dues are $40 a month.

"And that's it, friend. That's every red cent you'll pay for being an Alpha Cholera, except naturally $5.00 a month for the telephone, a quarter a day for hot water, and $300 for your handsome zircon Alpha Cholera pin. Of course there'll be special events from time to time, but we won't worry about those now, will we?"

"No," said Roger.

"Now that you know all the facts about Alpha Cholera, are you ready to make your decision?" Shylock asked. "We want you to go into this thing with your eyes open. This is the most important step you have ever taken in your life, and we don't want you to regret it. We want you to *want* to join Alpha Cholera; otherwise we don't want you. The decision is entirely up to you. We have acquainted you with the facts, and that is all we can do. Now, you take your time and think it over. We'll give you ninety seconds."

I knew it was an important decision, and I took the full allotted time. As they twisted my arms, I mentally weighed the considerations in the case. There was only one answer I could reasonably, honestly, and conscientiously give.

"I'll pledge," I said.

We shook hands silently all around, not trusting ourselves to speak.

"Shy," said Roger, after we had choked back our tears, "you tell him about the pledge period while I get everything ready for the ceremony." He left.

"Now," said Shylock, "you are going to be pledged in just a few minutes. For six months after that you are going to be a pledge. Then you get initiated and become what is called an active. During your pledge period you are sort of a little brother to the actives. You come to us with your problems and we give you advice about whatever you want to know. We choose your clothes and your girls for you. You just let us actives worry about every-thing."

I nuzzled against his sleeve. "There, there," he said quietly.

"All ready," called a voice from down the hall, and I left with Shylock for the pledging ceremony. (The ritual that followed is very secret, and I must ask the reader to keep the ensuing account in strictest confidence.)

We entered a room lit dimly by candles. A group of young men sat cross-legged in a circle on the floor. In the corner of the room on a dais Roger sat, dressed in a curiously inscribed robe. Frankincense and myrrh burned in an icon on the wall.

Shylock led me to the center of the circle. He chanted:

> *"I bring a man*
> *Into this clan."*

> *"Hubba, gubba,*
> *Goodrich rubba,"*

intoned the circle.

A barefoot maiden in a white gown entered bearing a young ram above her head. She deposited the ram in Roger's lap.

> *"Ram, bam,*
> *Thank you ma'am,"*

he said.

He drew a curiously inscribed kriss from his robe and slit the ram's throat. He dipped his finger in the blood and, beckoning me to the dais, made a curious inscription on my forehead.

"He's been washed in the blood of the ram," Roger announced.

"He's been washed in the blood of the ram," repeated the circle. Then they sang:

> *"Blood, thud,*
> *Fuddy dud."*

They leaped to their feet. Each put his hands on the hips of the one in front of him. They proceeded to move around me in a curious dance consisting of three steps and a kick, regularly repeated. After a while they resumed their positions and chanted:

> *"Simba, marimba,*
> *Richard himba."*

The lights went on, and suddenly their smiling faces were shaking my hand. Tears streamed uncheckable from my little eyes. "My brothers! My brothers!" I cried hoarsely.

Now I was on their shoulders, and they were giving three cheers and a tiger for me.

"By the way," said Shylock, "what's your name?"

"Asa Hearthrug," I answered.

"Oh, Jesus," he said.

CHAPTER VI

Je dormait dans un gros lit.—GORIOT

BUT ALL WAS NOT PLAY at the University of Minnesota. Now I began classes, and that was work—the good, satisfying work of learning.

I shall always remember the first class I attended. It was a class in sociology. I took a seat in the front row and spread my paper and pencils neatly on my desk. Turning to my brother students, I smiled friendlily. They threw lighted matches at me in a demonstration of good fellowship. Then the venerable white-haired professor entered the room. He advanced to the lectern at the head of the class. Putting on his pince-nez, he surveyed us for a moment. "Jeez," he said, "they get crumbier every year."

We laughed appreciatively.

"My name is Schultz," said the professor. "Now, get out paper and pencil, and I'll give you a list of books you'll need for this course. Ready? *Introduction to the Study of Sociology* by Schultz. *Sociology Made Simple* by Schultz. *Sociology for College Freshmen* by Schultz. *Survey of Freshman Sociology* by Schultz. *Sociology for Freshmen in College* by Schultz. *Introductory Monograph to the Study of Freshman Sociology* by Schultz. *Broader Aspects of Sociology* by Schultz. *Bibliography of Schultz's Treatises on Sociology for College Freshmen* by Schultz.

"I'll let you out of class early today so you can run right over to the bookstore and buy these books. And don't try to get them secondhand because you can't. I just wrote them this summer. Don't try to sell them when you're through, either. I'm writing a new set right now. You don't think I live on my salary here, do you? Why, the third-string fullback made more than I did last year.

"But enough of this pecuniary chitchat. Let's get down to business. This is a class in sociology. Now, what is sociology? I'll tell you what sociology is. Sociology is the study of how people live together."

I felt a prod in my ribs. Turning, I saw a dark-eyed, finely mustached girl in a close-knit burlap dress. "Hey," she whispered, "you know what sociology is?"

"The study of how people live together," I answered.

"Nah," she said. "It's the study of how the working class is oppressed under the capitalistic system."

The professor fixed us with a baleful eye. "If you two don't mind," he said, "I'll go on with my lecture."

"Tool," hissed the girl.

"In this course," continued the professor, "we shall study the various forms of communal life, the habits, customs, and mores, as we like to call them, that prevail among the different peoples of the world. After learning the broad backgrounds of the subject we shall take up the most important part of sociology. We shall study the individual from the standpoint of his environment. Sociology has proved that the key to individual behavior can be found in environment. For instance, last year we went through the records of the Minneapolis police department and compiled case histories of all the persons listed there. We found without exception that each one of them had come from what we call a 'bad' home or neighborhood.

"Let me cite a typical case, that of Mildred W., at present an inmate of the Effie T. Libidinous Home for Erring Girls.

"Mildred W. was one of twenty-seven children. Her father, Chauncey W., earned four dollars a week as a taper snuffer, but he seldom worked more than a week or two out of the year because of the meager demand for his talents. The mother was a laconic slattern named Bunny who spent the bulk of her time fretfully paring her nails. The family lived a peripatetic home life in the tender of a Baltimore & Ohio freight train.

"Aside from Mildred the children were generally a normal lot except for four boys, Primus, Secundus, Tertius, and Quartus, who were all joined together at the forehead, and Al, another son, who was six feet, nine inches tall, weighed thirty-five pounds, and spent his days boring holes in a table leg with his head.

"The rest of the children were as happy as children can be who don't eat. Chauncey W. tried to keep the children's minds off of food by organizing games. These were reasonably successful except when the children's attention lagged and they fell upon the youngest child and devoured it.

"Mildred never participated in these games. She was an adopted child, and although the family always tried to make her feel at home and never mentioned that she was adopted, she knew subconsciously that she was an outsider. While her sisters and brothers romped about, Mildred sat in a corner aimlessly cutting an old tarpaulin into isosceles triangles.

"In addition to her feeling that she did not belong, something else was troubling Mildred. She was ten years old at this time and beginning to pass through puberty. She asked her mother to explain the subtle changes that were coming over her, but her mother merely blushed and said, 'It ain't fitten to talk about.'

"Then one day Mildred picked up a circular advertising for peach pickers in California. In the dead of night she appropriated a shift, which was the family's sole article of clothing, and ran away to seek a job picking peaches.

"She met a girl named Frances Fagin on the highway. After hearing Mildred's plans, Frances said, 'Listen, honey, you're too pretty to pick peaches. You come with me and I'll show you how to get your mitts on some real dough.'

"That night Mildred and Frances met a couple of desperadoes, the notorious Nidrick brothers, Norman and Neville, and the four of them held up a Standard Oil station near Lima, Ohio, making off with $65 and a quart of Iso-Vis.

"They went to Davenport, Iowa, where they dissipated their swag in three months of riotous living. Finding themselves without funds, they knocked over the Farmers and Merchants Bank in Albert Lea, Minnesota. Their loot totaled $983,000,000. (There was an interesting side light to this robbery. The president of the Farmers and Merchants Bank, one Lawrence [Fats] Demijohn, was unable to satisfactorily explain how come he had so much money in his bank. Upon investigation it was learned that Demijohn, himself, had robbed the First Trust Company of Bismarck, North Dakota, the summer before and stored the loot in his own bank.)

"But I digress. Mildred decided not to share the proceeds with her accomplices. She drew a Luger that she had concealed in her tunic and dispatched the three of them.

Then she packed the money in a valise and caught a train East. On the train there was a mixup in bags and somebody walked off with Mildred's valise. Although she advertised in several papers, her valise was never returned to her. This had a profound effect on her personality. In her own words, 'I made up my mind right there and then never to trust nobody no more.'

"Mildred was now almost twelve years old and in the first flush of young womanhood. It was a simple matter for her to enter a brothel. She stayed there two years, finally leaving in a fit of pique when she discovered that the other girls were getting paid.

"For several weeks she wandered around hungry, keeping alive by snatching bread crumbs from irate pigeons. At length she found work dealing fan-tan in a Chinese joss house. Here she became acquainted with Norbert Huh, a narcotics peddler who put her to work selling hasheesh.

"Unfortunately, Mildred began sampling her wares. One night, while driving her car under the influence of hasheesh, she drove it right into the reading room of the public library and killed two mannish-looking women who were reading *The Well of Loneliness*.

"She was apprehended and convicted, but instead of being put in some dirty old prison, she was committed to a modern, homelike institution of correction. She is given a great deal of freedom and loving care. To help rehabilitate her, she is being taught handicraft. Mildred is responding very well. As soon as she promises to stop decapitating matrons with her crosscut saw she will be released to take her place in society.

"Well, that's all for today. Run along now and buy the books and tomorrow we'll plunge into the study of sociology."

I walked out of class with the girl who had spoken to me. We stopped in the hall while she rolled a cigarette and struck a match on her rope-soled shoe. The label on the sole said "Made in the Workers' Co-operative at Omsk."

"Well," I said, "it looks like sociology is going to be a lot of fun."

She spat obliquely across the hall and did not answer.

"My name is Asa Hearthrug," I said. "What's yours?"

"Call me Yetta Samovar. That's my Party name. I took the name of our great feminine martyr."

"Who was she?" I asked.

She looked contemptuously at me. "Oh, God—to mention a popular figure from the bourgeois religion-myth —don't you know who Yetta Samovar was? Oh well," she sneered, flicking my Alpha Cholera pin with a dirty-nailed forefinger, "what can you expect from a fraternity counter-revolutionist?"

"Madam," I cried, drawing myself up, "I shall not listen to any attack on my fraternity! They're all swell kids, and they're loads of fun."

"Fun! Fun!" she shrieked. "That's what you came to the University for. You're just like the rest of them. Well, have your fun now. The working class is getting damned good and tired of supporting your temple of hedonism on their scarred backs. You'll see the day when the likes of you have your fun in salt mines."

"Permit me to correct you," I remarked coldly. "I did not come to the University for fun. I came to learn how to write."

"*You* want to write! *You!* Tell me, have you suffered?"

"Well, yes," I confessed. "I get awful chafed in summer."

Yetta looked at me for a long time, then she took my hand in hers and spoke. "Friend," she said tenderly, "I spoke hastily. It is now evident that you are not a fascist. You are merely politically undeveloped. But that is dangerous, doubly dangerous because you are in a fraternity."

I raised my hand. "Say of me what you like, but I will not hear a word against Alpha Cholera."

"Asa, you must listen to me. I promise you you will thank me later for that which I am going to tell you now. Let me ask you a question. What does your fraternity do?"

"Do? Why, they listen to records and play bridge and hold dances and——"

"Exactly," she interrupted. "That's my point. They listen to records and play bridge and hold dances. Do they ever go out and join a picket line? Do they discuss ways and means to better the condition of the working class? Do they collect funds for the families of martyrs of the class war? No! No! No!"

"But that doesn't make them fascists," I protested.

"Ah," she screamed, "but it does! They are either for us or against us." Her tone grew softer. "Asa, you want to be a writer. What kind of writer do you want to be? Do you want to be a feeble, sniveling voice of decadent reaction or do you want to be the brave trumpet of a new era?"

"The brave trumpet of a new era," I said promptly.

"Then you must let me guide you. Tonight the Minnesota chapter of the Subversive Elements League is holding a meeting. Will you come with me?"

"Yes," I said simply.

"Good," she said. "I'll meet you at nine in front of the chemistry building. You won't regret it. And maybe later I can help you with your writing. I know a few people on *Poignancy,* the campus literary magazine."

"Oh, Yetta," I cried, "do you think you could——"

"We'll see," she said. "We'll see. Well, I'll meet you tonight."

"All right. Say, by the way, who was the original Yetta Samovar?"

"She was the first Soviet woman to operate a power crane," said Yetta. "One day while working at the Dnepropetrovsk dam she leaned out of her crane to wave a greeting to a young man whose bed she shared and with whom she had become quite friendly. She leaned too far. Down she plunged into a block of newly laid, quick-drying concrete. Her last words as the concrete hardened about her were, 'Solidarity forever!' "

"I see," I said.

CHAPTER VII

Je suis froid.—ROLLAND

YETTA WAS WAITING when I got to the chemistry building. "Come on," she said. "It's about a half mile from here. Let's run."

"Why?" I asked. "Are we late?"

"No, but you're a stranger. It will make a good impression if you come in smelling of sweat."

We loped to a basement apartment on the coal docks near the river. Inside were about fifteen or twenty young men and women sitting cross-legged on the floor. Their acne glowed dully in the glare of an unshaded light bulb that dangled from the ceiling. At the head of the room was an uncovered table. A hirsute fellow with thick glasses stood behind it.

Yetta found a place for us near the back of the room. She heaped up two little piles of coal dust, and we sat down.

The hairy fellow rapped on the table for order. "That's Sam Nihilism, our commissar," Yetta whispered.

"The meeting will now come to order," Sam said. "First, I want to introduce John Das Kapital and Natashya Fiveyearplan, who have been sent here by the central committee to handle publicity for us."

John and Natashya advanced to the table amid enthusiastic applause. John held up his hand. "Comrades," he began. "Comrade Natashya and I are going to help you with publicity this year. Last year we were at the University of Wisconsin where, I can say with all modesty, our work met with considerable success. We have ac-

44

quainted ourselves with the situation at Minnesota, and we find that it is quite similar to what we had to face at Wisconsin.

"Believe me, comrades, it was almost impossible to get any publicity at Wisconsin. The kept press refused to print any notices of our meetings or any accounts of our activities. It looked hopeless, but we finally got a story into the paper. Not just a little story, but a big story, and on the front page and with pictures."

There were admiring whistles and cries of "Pictures, yet!" from the audience. John smiled modestly and continued:

"Let me tell you how we did it. We scheduled a demonstration on the steps of the university library one afternoon. Natashya started to speak and pretty soon a few curious students collected. I waited for a little while, and then I ran to the dean's office. All out of breath I burst in and announced that communists were setting the library on fire. The dean got hold of the campus cop immediately and told him to rush to the library. As soon as Natashya saw the cop coming she threw herself to the steps, knocked out her front teeth, and screamed that she had been clubbed. In an instant a huge crowd appeared. Well, the paper simply couldn't ignore that story."

The audience applauded wildly. Natashya acknowledged the ovation with a proud toothless grin.

"That Natashya," Yetta whispered to me, "she's one of our best Party workers. She used to be in charge of our free love campaign, but since she knocked out all her front teeth she can't even give it away."

The two publicists retired, and Sam took over again. "Our next speaker needs no introduction. He has been in charge of our youth movement at the University of Minnesota for the last twenty-two years. You all know him—Westbrook Workingstiff."

A huge, bloated fellow of forty-odd years in a three-piece denim suit came up to the table. He began to read from a sheaf of paper in his enormous fist. "Fellow yoots, like we all know, da capitalistic system is doomeded. It is up to us, da yoot of America, to build da future. What

kinda future is it gonna be? Dat dere question it is up to you to answer it.

"We got to take t'ings in our own hands. Da gov'ment is full wit' corrupshun. Da forces of reaction is lurking all around us, waiting to grab us by our t'roat. Our enemies is crafty and unscrupuless. Dey'll give you dat sweet talk, but dey are a two face. Dey won't stop at not'ing to stem da tide of our movemint.

"We, da yoot of Minnesota, must be a inspiration to da rest of da yoot of da nation, and also a inspiration to da farmers and da rest of da working class. But we can be a inspiration only t'rough action. It is up to us, da yoot, to do some action.

"We, da yoot, must not be ascared of da battle. We must girdle our loins and go fort' wit'——"

He paused to turn a page. The thin sheet resisted his great blunt fingers. He fumbled and hacked at it vainly for several minutes. Sweat poured down his face. At last he abandoned the struggle. "T'ank you," he said, and stepped down.

Sam returned to the table. "How many of us who are active in the Movement are really familiar with the full significance of it? Do we really know what we are working for? Are we aware of the backgrounds of the class war? The next speaker is one who can enlighten us on these subjects. His topic is 'The Writings of Marx and Veblen.' I want to introduce our comrade and fellow student, Bruce Proletariat."

Bruce came forward and smiled in acknowledgment of the applause. When the hand clapping ceased he said, "I am proud and happy to be here tonight to talk to you about the writings of Marx and Veblen. I'm afraid, though, that my talk may be a little disappointing to some of you. You see, I had intended to do a lot of reading in Marx and Veblen during the last summer vacation, but I was so busy working at Daddy's bank that I really couldn't do all the reading I wanted to.

"As a matter of fact, I didn't get to read Veblen at all. But I did find out a few things about him. It will interest you to know that Veblen lived a good many years right here in our Minnesota."

There was a burst of applause. Bruce held up his hand. "And he married a girl from Northfield, Minnesota."

The applause grew louder, and some hats flew into the air.

"As for Marx"—his eyes twinkled slyly—"I can tell you this much. He wasn't one of the Marx brothers!"

The room echoed with appreciative laughter.

Bruce held up his hand. "But seriously, folks, I did read some of Marx, and it was mighty worthwhile reading, marx my words."

We howled until the tears came to our eyes.

"Well, a good laugh never hurt anybody," Bruce said. "But seriously, I want to recommend both Marx and Veblen to you. You will do well to read these two men so that you can become familiar with what we are fighting for.

"You know, a lot of our critics sneer and say that we college people don't even know what we are talking about. Well, you read Marx and Veblen and then let them try to say something like that. Just let them try. Then you can turn on them and give them tit for tat.

"I cannot stress too strongly the need for being well informed. Only if we, ourselves, know the facts can we hope to go out and educate others. I know that you are all busy with schoolwork and this and that, but try to set aside a little time each day for Marx and Veblen. Read one page a day, or half a page, if that's all you have time for. I'm not going to tell you it's light reading. It's not. It's awfully heavy. And I'm not going to stand here and pretend that I know what it's about. What I do is memorize it, and then when some reactionary fascist gets me in an argument I just give him a couple of pages of it point-blank and watch him run for cover.

"Marx and Veblen didn't write the only books on the subject. You should also read Herbert Spencer's *Decline of the West* and *Looking Backward* by Ralph Bellamy and many others. You can also find a good list of books in the Catholic Index. So don't try to make the excuse that you can't find a book to read because there are plenty.

"In conclusion let me recite a little slogan I made up on the way to the meeting tonight: 'The more books read, the quicker capitalism dead.' "

Bruce retired amid thunderous applause, and Sam returned. "The final speaker of the evening is Brenda Molotov. As you know, each summer we sponsor a summer camp for our members. Last summer Comrade Brenda was in charge of our camp, and she is going to tell you all about it."

A spavined, pock-marked girl stepped up. "Last summer we had our camp on beautiful Lac Qui Parle in northern Minnesota. We all had a real nice time. There were many healthful exercises and games, in addition to which we had many discussion groups and seminars concerning Marxian dialectics. We also had many interpretative dances. Also we had a communal garden in which we grew what we believed to be cabbage.

"In the evenings we built a camp fire around which we sat and had discussions and sang many songs, such as 'I'll Be Glad When You're Dead, You Industrialist, You' and 'Let the Bosses Take the Losses.' We also burned many prominent capitalists in effigy.

"We broke camp September first and went into New York Mills, a near-by town, where we picketed a church and broke the windows in the Chamber of Commerce. Although we all agreed that it was a very nice summer and we had many good times, we were also happy to come back to the University and carry on our work. Thank you."

When the applause had subsided Sam said, "Now we will sing 'Workers, Workers,' and the meeting will adjourn. On your way out you will find a collection box for contributions to descendants of martyrs of the Haymarket massacre."

We all stood and sang the stirring song, "Workers, Workers." I didn't know the words, but after the first rendition I, too, joined in the singing. Yetta's hand crept into mine as our voices joined.

"Workers, workers,
Don't be shirkers,
There's a job we have to do.
Flee your prison,
Collectivism
Is the thing for you and you.

"Don't be stooges.
Subterfuges
Is all the bosses ever give.
They make millions,
Sometimes billions,
But do they care how you live?

"Seize the power
At this hour,
Fight with all your mights and mains.
Strike the blow now,
Onward go now,
You have nothing to lose but your chains,
But your chains,
But your chains,
You have nothing to lose but your chains."

Yetta and I came from the crowded meeting room into the crisp autumn night. She put her hand beneath my arm and we walked silently along. Only our footsteps marred the stillness of the night, the hard tattoo of mine and the scuffing of her rope soles. Somehow I felt no need for words as I let myself be caressed by the velvet of the night and the presence of her.

Soon we were on the campus, serene in the pale moonlight. A pile of fallen leaves lay under a dark, stately oak. We sank into it with a sigh. She rolled a cigarette and lit it.

"Yetta," I said softly, "I've been a fool, a fool, an utter fool."

"Yes," she agreed.

"The meeting tonight has opened my eyes. I had no idea, Yetta, I didn't know."

She emitted smoke from her nostrils noncommittally.

"You're angry with me," I said, making a moue. "Please

don't be, Yetta. I didn't know about the forces of reaction. Honestly, I didn't. And now that I do, I want to fight them. I want to be one of you."

"Oh, you do," she said bitterly. "And how do you want to fight them?"

"I want to read books, and go to summer camps, and sing songs like all of you do."

"And what about your precious fraternity?"

What, indeed, about my fraternity? I picked up a leaf and slowly tore it to bits. "My fraternity is a force of reaction, huh?" I asked.

She laughed humorlessly. "What do you think?"

"Then I—I will give it up."

There. It was said.

She took my hands in hers. "Asa," she said with curious tenderness, "you are giving up a fraternity, but you are joining a greater fraternity, the fraternity of the downtrodden, the oppressed, the wage slaves. You will not regret it."

I looked deep into her eyes, noticing for the first time a cast in the left one. "I will not regret it, Yetta, if it will bring me closer to you." Suddenly words that had been forming in my heart since I first saw her cascaded out. "Yetta, you are of the true nobility, the nobility of heart. For you are of the world, and the world is you. When a Mexican *peso* bends over to glean beans your back aches for him. When an underpaid seamstress works all day in a sweatshop your eyes smart for her. When a Spanish peasant dies in the name of humanity your bell tolls for him. You are the soul, the one-ness, of mankind."

"I am?" she asked.

"Yetta— my darling, I know that we have met but today. Perhaps you think we have not known each other long enough for me to speak the way I must. But, no, you are not one to be concerned with the pettiness of time. What, then, is time? It is an invention of man, no more."

"Capitalists invented overtime," Yetta interjected.

"Let him who dwells on convention say what he will," I cried. "I am compelled to speak. Yetta, let me but love you. Let me serve you. Let me march by your side, uplifted in the glory of your eyes."

"Sure, Asa, sure," said Yetta.

We kissed.

A wondrous thing happened. In Minnesota, in October, I heard the song of a nightingale. "Did you hear it, Yetta?" I whispered.

"The nightingale? Yeah. There's a lot of them over in the medical building. They cut them open and pull out their pancreas. It contains a fluid that's supposed to be good for the bends."

We sat silent for a time. She rolled another cigarette. "Yetta," I said at length, "now that we're going steady, would you wear this?"

I removed my Alpha Cholera pin from my vest and held it before her.

"Bourgeois bauble," she smirked, snatching it from my hand and pinning it on her bodice.

"I'd like to pin it on," I said shyly.

"Sure you don't want to cop a feel?" she said suspiciously.

"Yetta!" I cried reproachfully.

But I did.

CHAPTER VIII

Asseyons-nous un moment à la terrasse.—DAUDET

WHEN I CAME into the Alpha Cholera house that night Roger and Shylock were sitting in the living room looking at Petty girls and licking their lips. They called hello to me, but I walked right past them without answering.

I went directly to my room and started to pack. In a few minutes Roger and Shylock burst in. "Say, what's the idea of not answering us downstairs?" Roger demanded.

"Begone, forces of reaction!" I cried.

"What's that?" exclaimed Shylock angrily. "Are you forgetting that you're a pledge in this fraternity?"

"I *was* a pledge. Now I am an active in the greater fraternity of mankind."

They circled me warily. "You been drinking," accused Shylock.

"Yes, drinking indeed. Drinking from the cup of love for my fellow man, drinking the bitter draught of human oppression."

"Where you been tonight?" said Roger.

"If you must know, I've been to a meeting of the Subversive Elements League. Now, are you satisfied?"

They looked relieved. "Oh, no wonder you're talking like you are," Roger said. "An evening with those icks would make anybody crazy."

"Please!" I cried. "I will not listen to you slander my fellow toilers in the cause of liberation."

Shylock took Roger's arm and led him to the corner of the room where they whispered for a short time. They came back smiling amiably.

54

"We're sorry, Asa. We didn't mean to make you mad," said Roger. "Tell me, how'd you happen to go to that meeting tonight?"

"I was invited."

"By whom, Asa?" asked Shylock gently.

"I'd rather not say," I replied coldly.

"Are you ashamed to tell, Asa?" Roger teased.

"Ashamed! Proud, rather. Yetta Samovar is the finest young woman I know," I said stoutly.

"See? What did I tell you," Shylock said to Roger.

"Yetta Samovar. I know her," Roger said. "Cockeyed broad with a mustache."

"Hers is the true beauty of soul and compassion," I said haughtily.

"A Red," Roger continued. "Wants to destroy the American institutions of democracy and freedom."

I laughed bitterly. "Freedom! Freedom to be enslaved by the capitalistic masters. Freedom to——"

"Asa!" Roger interrupted harshly. "Now you listen to me for a minute. Come over here by the window." His tone grew softer. "Look at it, Asa. There it is. The University of Minnesota, calm, strong, peaceful. An American institution, Asa, built by Americans to educate American youth in the American way of life.

"And look below you on the street. See the people, some driving in American cars built by American workmen in American factories, others walking, enjoying an American evening. They are free, Asa, free to ride or to walk, to work or to play, to do whatever they like in the good old, common-sense American manner.

"And who wants to destroy this American way of life? The people you were with tonight. And why? Oh, I know, they tell you they want to liberate the working class and all the rest of their filthy Red lies, but that isn't the reason. They want to destroy because they are warped, bitter, unhappy. And why are they warped, bitter, and unhappy? I'll tell you why."

He paused thirty seconds for emphasis. *"Because they can't get into a fraternity."*

Now Shylock put his arm around me. "That's right, Asa," he said. "Not a fraternity on campus will have them. And the sororities won't take their girls. That's why they'll tell you that fraternities and sororities are the forces of reaction. Frustration, simple frustration. Sour grapes.

"Why, you and I know that fraternities are as American as apple pie. What could be more democratic than a group of fine young men living together, sharing each other's problems, enjoying each other's company, working together for the good of all? And the most democratic thing of all about fraternities is the privilege to select whom it wants and reject whom it doesn't want. Why, that's the very basis of democracy. How would it be if just anyone who wants to be President walked right into the White House and sat down at the desk and said he was President? What a fine state of affairs that would be.

"And I suppose they told you that fraternities don't have any social consciousness. Well, you just go back and tell them that every Christmas our own Eino Ffliiik-kiinnenn plays Santa Claus at the Sara K. Malnutrition Foundling Home. See what they have to say to that."

"Eino Ffliiikkiinnenn himself is a good illustration of democracy in action," said Roger. "Four years ago he was an unknown boy roaming around the North Woods precariously keeping body and soul together by stealing bait from bear traps. Then a Minnesota football scout saw him, lassoed him, put shoes on him, taught him to sign his name, and brought him to the University to play football. And last year Eino Ffliiikkiinnenn was an All-American. An All-*American!*"

"Let's go downstairs. I want to show you something," Shylock said.

We went into the living room. He pointed at the well-stocked bookshelves that lined one wall. "I suppose they told you to read books too. Well, if you can't live without reading books we've got plenty of red-blooded American literature right here. Complete Rex Beach, everything he ever wrote. Autographed too. Zane Grey, Edgar Rice Burroughs, Max Brand, Lloyd C. Douglas, and many others. Plus we've got bound volumes of interesting and entertaining periodicals like the *Saturday Evening Post, Esquire,* and, if you go in for heavier stuff, *Cosmopolitan.*"

Roger was putting a record in the phonograph. "Listen," he said.

I snapped to attention. It was Kate Smith singing "God Bless America." My eyes smarted with unspilled tears, and a lump filled my throat. Not until several minutes after the record had stopped playing did I trust myself to speak. "Can you ever forgive me?" I choked.

They each took one of my hands. "It's all right, Asa," said Roger.

"Sure," said Shylock.

"Maybe it's a good thing this happened," Roger mused. "Now you really know what fraternity means."

"Oh, I do. I do!" I cried.

"You must promise never to see those people again," said Shylock.

"I promise," I said simply.

"And that girl, that Yetta Samovar, you'll have to give her up," said Roger.

"If—if you say so," I replied.

"Now don't look so glum," chided Shylock. "We'll get you a girl, and a darn smooth one, don't you worry. She'll be a good American sorority girl."

"Say, Shy," said Roger, "maybe we can get Asa a date for the Beta Thigh party Saturday night."

Shylock snapped his fingers. "I'll bet we can. What time is it? Is it too late to call their house?"

Roger looked at his watch. "Not even two."

Shylock left to make the call. "Beta Thigh is the best sorority on campus," Roger explained. "We have a dating arrangement with them. We take care of their extra girls and they take care of our extra fellows. And if one of our fellows has a girl in from out of town she stays at the Beta Thigh house, and we accommodate any out-of-town fellow who comes to visit a Beta Thigh. Just another example of good old American working together."

"I've been such a fool, Roger," I said. "I wish I could thank you for all you've done for me tonight."

"You can thank us best by being a good Alpha Cholera, Asa. You must remember now that your actions do not reflect on you alone, but on all of us. In the true democratic tradition, being an Alpha Cholera entails not only

privileges, but obligations. The pin you are wearing——
By the way, where is your pin?"

"Oh, ah, er, eh, I left it up in my room."

"You must wear it constantly, Asa," he said with gentle
reproachfulness. "The pin you should be wearing is a
standard, an emblem of Alpha Cholera and all it stands
for, and as long as you wear that pin you must do nothing
to make Alpha Cholera ashamed of you."

Shylock returned from the phone. He slapped my back.
"You lucky dog, I got you a date with as smooth a little
number as you'll ever want to meet. Her name is Noblesse
Oblige. You be at the Beta Thigh house at nine-thirty
Saturday night. It's a song-title party. You come dressed
to represent the title of a popular song. There'll be a prize
for the best costume. Those crazy kids always think up
some clever stunt."

A sense of shame and penitence swept over me, so
strong that I thought I should not bear it. "Thank you,
thank you," I cried in a strange voice.

Looking neither to the right nor to the left, I walked
stiffly to the stairs and ascended. As I reached the top
they called me. I turned around.

"Good night," they said. They were smiling.

I ran blindly to my room.

CHAPTER IX

Ouvrez la fenêtre.—ZOLA

I DECIDED TO GO to the Beta Thigh song-title party as "Tea for Two." It took a great deal of practice to master my costume, which was a tea service for two balanced on my head, but when I finally walked up to the door of the Beta Thigh house on Saturday night I carried myself with all the aplomb of an African laundress.

I rang the bell. A gray-haired, matronly woman opened the door. "How do you do?" I said. "I'm Asa Hearthrug, and I've come to the party. I am the guest of Noblesse Oblige."

"Come right in, Asa. I'm Mother Bloor, the house mother. You sit right down here on the sofa and I'll go call Noblesse."

Mother Bloor was back in a few minutes. "She'll be down right away. She's fixing her costume. Well, Asa, you look like a nice boy," she said, putting her hand on my knee.

I smiled modestly.

"You got any older brothers?"

"No ma'am," I said.

"Your father ain't a widower, is he?"

"Not when I left him, he wasn't."

"Uh. You thought any about getting married?"

"Some," I admitted.

"Well, let me tell you, boy, you could do a lot worse than marrying some nice mature woman that knows how to cook and take care of a house and what a man likes. Get me?" She nudged me and winked.

"Madam!" I cried.

"I tell you, these young puss ain't got any idea of how to treat a man. Oh, sure, they're pretty to look at, but you mark my words, you'll soon get sick of looking at 'em. A man needs a nice mature woman. Well, here comes Noblesse now. You think over what I said. I'm home all the time."

A slender girl in a two-piece gown with an exposed midriff approached. I could not see her face because it was enveloped in a cloud of black smoke that rose from a smudge pot that was cunningly hinged to her navel.

"This is Asa Hearthrug, Noblesse Oblige," said Mother Bloor.

"How do you do?" I said.

"Oh, Asa," she cried in an enchanting little voice like the tinkle of a silver bell, "I think your costume is simply marvy, I mean actually. I mean it's so clever, after all, it's just grand I mean. 'Tea for Two.' How did you ever think of it, I mean really?"

"Shucks," I said, "it's not half as clever as yours. 'Smoke Gets in Your Eyes,' isn't it?"

"Oh, you guessed!" she cried, making a little moue.

"Why don't you children go in and dance?" Mother Bloor suggested.

Noblesse took my arm and we went into the amusement room of the house where several couples were dancing to the music of an automatic phonograph. "Isn't Mother Bloor keen?" asked Noblesse as we walked. "I mean after all, she's just like a real mother to us girls."

"Yes," I said.

We got on the dance floor just as a Benny Goodman record started to play. "Oh, B.G.!" cried Noblesse. "Next to T.D. I like him best. He carves me. I mean he carves me. Does he carve you?"

"Yes," I said, "he carves me."

"Me too," she breathed. "Man, he's murder, Jack."

The next record was a Glenn Miller. "G.M!" whooped Noblesse. "Man, what solid jive, I mean he's rcct. Have you heard his disc of 'Fell Me, Woodsman, with a Snag-Toothed Saw?' "

"No," I said.

"Awful fine slush pump, I mean awful fine. You ought to dig that."

The next record was a Guy Lombardo waltz. Noblesse stopped dancing. "That G.L.," she said, "strictly a square, I mean after all, he's an Ed. Let's go out on the porch and sit down."

I was quite willing because my groin was a mass of first-degree burns from pressing against her smudge pot.

On the veranda, which had been imaginatively decorated with Japanese lanterns and festoons of crepe paper, young couples sat around and smoked and chatted pleasantly. Noblesse spied some friends over in a corner. "Let's go sit with those kids. They're loads of fun," she said.

When we reached them Noblesse introduced me. "This is Asa Hearthrug—Bob Scream and Peggy Orifice."

"How do you do?" I said.

"Hi, Asa, what do you sasa?" Bob yelled jovially. We chuckled appreciatively.

"What darling costumes you kids have on," said Peggy.

"Thank you," Noblesse replied. "But I don't see yours."

Peggy opened her mouth. A cuckoo, cunningly attached to a pivot tooth, came out and crowed three times.

" 'Three O'clock in the Morning!' " cried Noblesse. "How clever, I mean how utterly."

"Wait'll you see mine," Bob boomed. "Hey, c'mere," he called to a figure that stood in the shadows. An elderly man dressed in a shirt of wide, vertical black-and-white stripes, a pair of white knickers, and athletic shoes, with a whistle on a string hung around his neck, came over to Bob. " 'My Reverie,' " Bob screamed. "Get it? Referee—reverie. Get it? Referee—reverie."

After our laughter had subsided Noblesse whispered to me, "That Bob, he's terribly clever. I mean he writes all the varsity shows on the campus. I mean I don't know where he thinks up all those gags year after year, I mean after all. He's thinking of enrolling in the University next year."

"I'm glad you kids came," said Peggy, tucking the cuckoo back in her cheek. "We were just having a serious discussion, and we'd like to ask the opinion of you kids about something. I had a coke date with Harvey Vacillate —he's a Sigma Phlegm—this afternoon, and he asked my advice about something. Harvey and I are platonic like that. We just go out on coke dates and ask each other's advice about our problems, and we have helped each other a good deal in the past. But this afternoon he asked me a question, and I mean, I just didn't know what to answer."

"I went on a coke date with him yesterday," said Noblesse. "I'm platonic with him that way, too, I mean. He's platonic with Sally Gelt and Wilma Urbane in our sorority too. Then he's platonic with some Chi Havoc girls too. But what was it he asked you?"

"Well," Peggy said, "he asked me if I thought that intelligent young women should observe the double standard."

"Did you hear about the girl who thought the double standard was two filling stations?" roared Bob.

"Now, Bob," chided Peggy gently, "the double standard is not a subject to joke about. It's a very burning issue of our times."

"Yes," agreed Noblesse. "I mean it's very important. After all, why shouldn't intelligent young people get together and discuss this problem? I mean this is the twentieth century, and women are supposed to be liberated; why shouldn't they have all the freedom that a man has?

"I don't mean that people should be promiscuous, I mean with just anybody. I mean after all there is a limit. And of course I mean all women shouldn't be allowed all this freedom—not until they've had certain advantages and shown themselves to be capable of freedom, I mean.

"I mean that sort of thing has to be done with a certain amount of *savoir faire,* and I say when a woman has been educated and has had advantages, after all she should be allowed to do what she wants."

"A woman like you, for instance," Bob shrieked slyly.

"Well, yes," said Noblesse. "I mean I think I'm intelligent enough not to have my conduct governed by what people did hundreds of years ago."

"Oh, you are, Noblesse, you are," I said.

"Everybody down to the dance floor," called a voice from the end of the porch. "The prize for the best costumes is going to be awarded."

We went back to the dance floor and marched in a line past the judge's stand. Mother Bloor was the judge. When the last couple had gone by Mother Bloor looked over the notes she had been taking and at length announced the winner.

"Noblesse Oblige and Asa Hearthrug."

Suddenly I was up at the front of the room with Noblesse, and all around us was a sea of smiling faces, blurred through my tears. "I can't believe it, I can't believe it," I kept repeating to Noblesse.

"We've won, Asa," she said, taking my hand. "I mean we've won."

Then Mother Bloor, smiling broadly, was putting a silver cup in my hand. "Don't forget it what I told you before," she whispered in my ear.

Now everyone was about us shouting cheery greetings, extending congratulations. I could only mouth brokenly, but Noblesse, cool and serene, spoke graciously for both of us until, at length, the well-wishers had gone.

"Whew," said Noblesse. "I mean I'm glad that's over. Let's take off our costumes and go get some air."

She disengaged the smudge pot from her navel. I saw her face for the first time. She was incredibly lovely. Her crisp brown hair was worn in a jaunty feather bob. Her blue eyes were pools of innocence. Her little nose was pert and saucy. Her mouth, adorned with fashionably dark lipstick, could only be described as kissable. I took the tea tray off my head and followed her into the garden.

We sat on a bench under a spreading banyan tree and lit cigarettes. "Are you having a good time, Asa?" she asked.

"Good!" I cried. "Say, better, marvelous."

"Isn't Bob funny?"

"Devastating," I said.

"You should see him when he puts a lampshade on his head. I mean you could die."

"I can imagine," I said, chuckling.

We smoked silently for a moment. "Noblesse," I said

64

slowly, "all this, these people, this trophy we won, this social grace, I never believed such things existed outside of storybooks."

She laughed silverly. "Yes, it's all true. And it's all the more enjoyable because"—her voice grew more serious —"because we know how to enjoy it. I mean we are the people who belong. After all, there are belongers and non-belongers. We are the belongers."

"Belongers and non-belongers," I said thoughtfully. "Yes, you've hit it, Noblesse. I want to belong to all of this, and—and most particularly I want to belong to you." I took her cool white hand in mine.

She allowed me to hold it for a moment, and then withdrew it. "Do you like football, Asa? I mean I'm crazy about it, I mean simply mad."

"Yes," I said.

"The season opens next Saturday, and I'm just dying to go, I mean actually. But nobody can get a ticket. I mean you really have to *rate* to get a ticket."

A thought struck me. "Noblesse, will you come to the game with me next Saturday?"

"With you? But where will you get a ticket, Asa?"

"Eino Ffilliikkiinnenn is a fraternity brother of mine," I said simply.

"Eino Ffilliikkiinnenn!" she exclaimed.

"Yes," I said modestly.

"Oh, Asa, I'd love to."

Her hand stole back into mine. "Noblesse," I said, "I don't know quite how to say this, and I know I shouldn't, but I must speak. Am I then made of stone? Noblesse, I shall not bandy words. I—I love you."

"Asa!" she cried. "I mean after all."

"Stay," I said. "Hear me out. I know we have met only this night, but what does love know of time? My heart is my clock and my calendar, and it ticks inexorably that I love you. If I had known you a million years I should only know what I know now: that you are beautiful and as wise as beautiful and gracious and pure and strong and good. Do not speak to me of time, for time is but a picayune in our world, yours and mine. Noblesse, say that you are mine."

"I mean you mean go steady?"

"Yes," I said simply, and I saw the answer in her eyes. Then she was in my arms, my mouth drinking the ambrosia of her lips.

"But we mustn't tell anybody. I mean we must keep it a secret," she said.

"Our secret," I breathed.

"How fun!" she cried, and clapped her hands. She extended her palm toward me. "The pin."

"The pin? Oh. Oh yes, the pin. I—I left it at the jeweler's to have some more diamonds put in. I'll have it for you Saturday."

"You sure?" she said, frowning.

"As sure, Noblesse, as my love for you."

She smiled. We kissed.

"I am so happy," I said. "Now I can be one of you and join your fun and your serious discussions too."

"Yes," she said. "They're very important. We had some very nice serious discussions tonight, didn't we, Asa?"

"Oh yes," I said. "That was very interesting about the double standard. Tell me, Noblesse, did you mean all you said about the double standard?"

She drew herself up. "Of course. I mean I meant every word of it. I mean after all, I don't just talk to hear myself talk, I mean."

"That's all I wanted to know," I said. I started to divest myself of encumbering garments.

She screamed and ran into the house.

Mother Bloor emerged from behind the banyan tree. "It's like I told you," she said. "You ought to get yourself a nice mature woman."

CHAPTER X

Donnez-moi le fromage.—CELINE

I NEXT saw Yetta Samovar in a psychology class. The instructor was lecturing on learning. "Learning," he said, "is the explanation for many of the things we erroneously call instincts. Even our most fundamental reactions are often not instinctive, but learned. I wish I could demonstrate this fact to you, but unfortunately we are not allowed to because of an untoward occurrence a few years ago.

"Dr. Pavlov, of the psychology department, was performing an experiment to show that so-called instincts are learned. He wheeled a little baby boy out on the lecture platform. 'This is little Terence, age six months,' he said. 'Using little Terence, I am going to prove to you that at six months an infant has not yet *learned* to be afraid.'

"One after the other, Dr. Pavlov put rats, snakes, tarantulas, lizards, scorpions, octopi, and dismembered corpses in little Terence's buggy. Little Terence cooed peacefully throughout the whole demonstration, completely unafraid.

"When little Terence's mother later learned what had happened, she stove in Dr. Pavlov's head with a jack handle. A Hennepin County jury acquitted her in a rising verdict.

"Learning," continued the instructor, "is not only the answer to the problems of instincts. Often learning can explain even the most complex conduct. I am in mind of the case of a young woman, Patricia S., a graduate of the

University of Minnesota, who was perfectly normal in every respect except one: every twenty-five seconds she yelped, leaped in the air, and screamed '$C_{10}H_{13}NO_2$.'

"Nobody thought anything of it for sveral years, but finally a friend persuaded Patricia to go to a psychoanalyst. After a lengthy, comprehensive examination the psychoanalyst discovered the cause of her peculiar actions. It seems that while she was at the University she took a course in pharmacy. One day, as she was bending over her worktable compounding phenacetin, of which $C_{10}H_{13}NO_2$ is the formula, a playful lab assistant goosed her. It had a profound effect upon her."

At the conclusion of the lecture I met Yetta in the hall. We sat down on the steps. "Yetta," I began slowly, "there's something I have to tell you."

"There's something I have to tell you, too, comrade," she said, rolling a cigarette. "I've gotten you appointed to our sedition committee."

"That's real nice, Yetta. But now you must listen to me. This isn't easy for me, believe me. I have been lying awake nights trying to think of another way to do it. But there is only one way—the quick, honest, decisive way. Any other way would be infinitely more painful."

"There's something else I wanted to tell you," she interrupted. "Now what was it? I'll think of it in just a minute."

"First I want you to know that you are one of the finest girls I have ever met," I said. "My admiration for you is boundless. I think that the way you work for your cause—which for *you* is the true cause—is commendable. I believe you to be utterly sincere, and sincerity is a virtue all too rare in these troubled times."

"I'll be damned," she said, "if I can remember it. It was something important too. Well, I'll think of it in a minute."

"But there are two kinds of people," I continued, "the belongers and the non-belongers. It is difficult—yea, impossible—to get them to understand one another. The belongers work in one direction and the non-belongers in the opposite. Nor can one be a renegade and desert one's faction. Yetta, I am a belonger, and you——"

"I got it," she exclaimed. "I've arranged an audition for you in the *Poignancy* office this afternoon."

"Poignancy!" I cried, for it was my fondest dream.

"Yes. The editor is listening to contributions this afternoon. Go on home now and get your best manuscript. Meet me at the publications building at one o'clock, and I'll take you to the *Poignancy* office, and you can read the manuscript."

"Yetta," I said quietly, a crooked smile on my face, "a moment ago I was going to say something for which I would have been sorry the rest of my life."

"You better hurry and get your manuscript. It's getting late." She stood up. "I've got to distribute some leaflets now. I'll see you at one."

I rushed home and rummaged through a trunk of my manuscripts. At last I decided on a tender story of young love called *Men Are Like That.* I remembered how Lodestone had liked that one when I had read it to her the summer before. For a moment I thought of Lodestone. Poor Lodestone. What a world of difference between us now. How quickly I had outgrown Lodestone. Little innocent. She knew nothing of the forces at work in the world, of belonging or not belonging. Hers was an uncomplicated world. It had been my world, too, I admitted to myself, but the University had changed all that. Now I was coming into my own, I was realizing my potentialities, my personality was rounding out. Already it was clear to me that until you knew the world you could not know yourself. I hastened to meet Yetta.

She arrived at the publications building punctually at one. "Come on," she said. I followed her into the building where the *Minnesota Daily,* the *Ski-U-Mah,* and *Poignancy* were published.

It was like walking into a movie set. Young men with hats on the backs of their heads and cigarettes dangling from their mouths rushed back and forth screaming "Hold the presses!" or "Leave me to a phone!" Lissome girls sat on desks, their silken legs dazzlingly extended, chain smoking and yelling "Hell" and "Damn" at frequent intervals. Nobody spoke below a shriek or was without a cigarette for a moment. One fellow, apparently someone of authority, sat in his shirt sleeves next to a telephone, screaming at the top of his lungs and punctuating his remarks with dangerous thrusts of a long-bladed shears. The phone rang. He put the receiver between his shoulder and his ear. "Rewrite," he bellowed. He scribbled for a few minutes, slammed the receiver back on the hook, and yelled, "Tear out page one! Just got the dope on the officer election of the Audubon Club."

"This is the office of the student newspaper, the *Minnesota Daily*. Come along," Yetta said.

We left this scene of derring-do and proceeded down the hall. We passed a door out of which came peal after peal of riotous laughter. "*Ski-U-Mah*," Yetta explained. "Campus humor magazine. They're reading their own stuff in there."

Then we entered a small office illuminated only by the light of a twenty-watt cerise bulb in a wall icon. When my eyes were accustomed to the light I made out the figure of a huge, hairy, anthropoid fellow sitting at a desk in the front of the room and a thin young woman and a swarthy young man sitting on a bench at the side.

"This is Asa Heathrug, Simian Gibbon," said Yetta, introducing me to the fellow at the table. "Simian is the editor of *Poignancy*."

"I'm so happy to know you," I said.

"Sit down on the bench," he growled. "I'll hear you in a little while. Who's next?"

I sat down with Yetta. The thin girl stood up. "I'm Cynthia Soul," she said. "I'd like to read some of my poetry. I have here a series of three poems which I call *The Oestrus Cycle*." She cleared her throat and began to read:

"Number one. *Tread Quietly, Al*.

> "*Tread quietly, Al,*
> *For the moon is a half slice of lemon*
> *On the teacup of the world,*
> *Quietly, quietly.*
> *Among the alien dolomites*
> *Slumbers one unsleeping*
> *And his name is Now*

"Number two. *Hold That Tiger.*

"Four young men were lined up against a wall and
*   shot this morning.*
And the cosmic eye turned
In oblique perpendicularity.

"Number three. *The Scent of an Ancient Rose.*

"Gamboling, gamboling.
In the absence of presence of nothing
Unbeing, uncreated, inchoate
Like the slash of a knife
Through the butter of eternity."

She stopped and waited for Simian to pass judgment.
"Too intelligible," he rumbled. "Everyone will know what
you're saying. What kind of poetry is that? Try again
sometime."

She left sadly. The swarthy one stood up. "I'm Francis
Sheboygan, an exchange student from Armenia," he said.
"I write plays in the New Thought manner. I am working
on a revolutionary play right now. Instead of speaking lines
in this play, the characters merely sniff meaningfully on
benzedrine inhalers. But I've brought something a little
more conventional to read today. It's called *Across the
Street on Tuesday Evening.* This play is set in a men's room
of a planetarium. As the play opens a three-fingered Negro
named Everyman is lackadaisically mopping the floor and
singing a mournful Estonian ballad in a minor key. He
sings in the original Estonian. The door opens stage left
and Abraham Lincoln comes in. 'How long do you think
a man's legs ought to be, Mr. Lincoln?' asks Everyman.

" 'Why, long enough to reach the ground, my boy,' says
Lincoln.

" 'That's the most beautiful thing I ever heard in my
life,' replies Everyman, and resumes his singing. Lincoln
assumes a nonchalant stance stage left and does a few
laconic birdcalls. The door opens, and a girl, known starkly
as Girl, enters. 'Whuffo you doin' in heah?' asks Everyman.
'Dis is a men's room.'

71

"Girl laughs bitterly. 'I can't read. I never had no schooling.'

" 'My poor child,' says Lincoln, abandoning his bird-calls.

" 'Mr. Lincoln!' cries Girl, new hope in her dead eyes. 'You're a big man. Can they shut off my water?'

"Lincoln smiles sadly. 'Yes, my child.' She begins to cry. Lincoln strokes her hair. 'Don't you care, dearie,' he says. An ice-cream vendor enters stage right. 'Give her a chocolate cone,' Lincoln says.

"The vendor laughs bitterly. 'They cut off my cones,' he says. Everyman pulls out a harmonica and softly plays 'They Cut Off My Cones.' Girl does a soft-shoe dance completely out of time with Everyman's music. Four unemployed puppeteers enter stage left and tacitly begin pitching pennies against the wall. 'I'll be back,' says Lincoln quietly, exiting stage right.

"A man made up as a dollar sign enters stage left. He pulls one hundred and twenty feet of foolscap from his tunic. 'I have an eviction order,' he says. He reads, 'Whereas and whereas and whereas.' Everyone slinks off the stage. A young man enters stage right. 'Know where I can locate a party named Harris or Benuti?' he asks.

" 'Whereas and whereas and whereas,' says Dollar Sign. The young man slinks off stage left. A cowboy enters stage right. He carries an ivory-headed cane. 'Whereas and whereas and whereas,' says Dollar Sign. The cowboy pulls a bowie knife and begins to whittle the ivory-headed cane.

" 'Whereas and whereas and whereas,' says Dollar Sign.

" 'You know,' says the cowboy, 'the little people are kind and good and gentle and beautiful.' The rest of the cast enters timorously from stage left and right. The cowboy continues, 'The little people may be little, but they're people.' Everyman pulls out a harmonica and softly plays 'In the Hall of the Mountain King.' The cowboy goes on, 'It takes a heap of livin' to make a people little. The little people have a dream, and in this dream somebody is saying a word to them. It sounds something like "phlox" or "labial," but it isn't. The little people know it isn't, and someday they are going to know what it is. Someday. Someday.'

"Dollar Sign trembles. Five provost marshals enter stage

right and clap him in irons. Lincoln descends from the ceiling on a guy rope. Gathering a heap of cedar chips, the cast builds a little fire. They vivaciously roast marshmallows. The curtain falls."

Simian considered. "It ain't bad, but it needs a little more symbolism. You take it home and work on it."

Francis Sheboygan left. I stood up.

"What you got? More poetry or plays?" asked Simian.

"No sir," I said. "I have a short story."

"All right. I could use a good robust short story. Go ahead."

"The title is 'Men Are Like That.' "

"It stinks," pronounced Simian. "But go ahead. I'll change it later."

I read, "Stephen walked up the path that lay coiled and fretted around the arbor."

"Stop!" he shouted. "Stephen! Of all the petit bourgeois, *Ladies' Home Journal* names in the world, that is the number one. And what kind of path around what kind of arbor? What kind of a counter-revolutionist are you? You better beat it, kid. You're wasting my time."

Yetta interceded. "Wait a minute, Simian. Those are only minor points. You can change the name of the character. Call him Sam."

"That's a good name," admitted Simian.

"And you can change the locale," she continued. "Give it a proletarian setting."

"An alley," said Simian. "That's it. O.K., go ahead, kid."

"The oblique rays of the afternoon sun silhouetted his broad shoulders, his flat hips, his long, lean legs, his finely molded head."

"Naaah," said Simian. "What kind of a body is that for a proletarian character? Here is a guy named Sam in an alley. He is shriveled up, hunchbacked. He got rickets because the capitalist bosses raised their prices on food and his mother couldn't get him the proper vitamins when he was a baby. Now he is bitter. He can't find work because he is a cripple. He hasn't got money to eat. He is going down the alley—I got it— searching in garbage cans."

"Sensational," Yetta said. "A graphic indictment of the system."

"Go ahead, kid," said Simian.

"Now Amelia came toward him trippingly, trippingly. Amelia of the golden hair, Amelia of the tawny green eyes, with her white, diaphanous dress, as pure as her soul, billowing in a gentle breeze."

"Amelia!" shrieked Simian. "Amelia yet. That's enough, kid. Get out of here. Get goin'."

"Wait," said Yetta. "You can call her Sarah."

"So all right, Sarah. So how comes by this scavenger a girl with golden hair, tawny eyes, a diaphanous white dress? What kind of diaphanous? You better get out, kid."

"So put a different kind of dress on her," said Yetta. "It's just a minor change."

"Everything is by you a minor change," said Simian. "All right, I'll call her Sarah, I'll dress her in torn, dirty bed ticking. But what is she doing in the alley?"

"Can't she be picking garbage too?" Yetta asked.

Simian looked interested. "That's it. She's a scavenger too. Sam opens up a garbage can, and there she is inside of it. She's a dwarf. At first he snarls at her. He's mad because she's cutting in on his garbage, see? Then he notices that it's a girl. Now another emotion comes over him. *Passion*. Go ahead, kid."

" 'My darling!' she said. 'At last you've come.' "

"No talking," said Simian. "Passion."

"He took the delicate contour of her cheek in his bronzed palm. The coolness of her lips was near, inviting. They kissed."

"What kind of bronzed palm? What kind of kissing? They been eating garbage. How can they stand to kiss? Listen. He lunges at her. She ducks. He lunges again. She whips out a bread knife from her tunic. All right. Go ahead, kid."

"She pressed his broad chest with firm gentleness. 'No,' she whispered, 'we mustn't.' "

"That's a pip," sneered Simian. "This guy is out for blood and she tells him he mustn't. Naaah, you better get out of here, kid."

"Wait," said Yetta; "you can make a few changes."

"Aaaah, well, all right. He's coming at her. She swings the knife. She slashes his arm. He belts her in the head. She falls back. He grabs her. She kicks him in the crotch. He falls back. Go ahead, kid."

"He smiled his crooked little smile. His eyes crinkled at the corners the way they did when she first saw him and lost her heart. 'Then this is good-by?' he breathed."

"Good-by is right," snarled Simian, "and he ain't got much breathing left either. She closes in on him. He's groggy. She jabs the knife into his throat. He falls. But when he falls he grabs her legs and she goes down. She cracks her head on a rock. She's groggy. He's just about gone. With his last ounce of strength he grabs the knife from her hand and lets her have it four times in the groin. They're both dead. Get the irony? They kill each other when they should be in the class war killing the other side."

"Powerful," said Yetta. "Powerful."

"Go ahead, kid. Let's hear the end."

"He turned. Slowly, erectly, he walked down the path. It started to rain."

"Naaah," said Simian. "What kind of walking? He's a dead pigeon. Listen. I got it. A capitalist banker walks past. He sees their bodies. He calls a policeman stooge. 'These people owe me money,' he says. 'Take them to the tallow works and have them rendered. Turn over the proceeds to me.' Then he turns and walks away. His footsteps echo hollowly in the distance."

"What a story!" said Yetta. "What an indictment! I told you Asa was a find."

"Maybe I can do something with him," Simian admitted. "You make those changes I suggested and come back."

We walked down the hall from the *Poignancy* office. They were still laughing in the *Ski-U-Mah* office. At the *Daily* the rewrite man was yelling, "Tear out the front page! I just got the results of the intramural chess matches."

CHAPTER XI

Mon oncle est mort.—BALZAC

I HAD SOME DIFFICULTY getting tickets for the football game from Eino Ffliiikkiinnenn. He didn't come around the fraternity house much because he was so busy with training. I finally found him eating with the team at their training table. A corps of waiters were lined against the wall, not serving the team, but watching so they didn't eat each other. Because I was his fraternity brother, Eino sacrificed two tickets behind the goal posts to me for $45.

Noblesse picked me up before the game. She was with Bob Scream and Peggy Orifice in Bob's convertible. There was a little time before the kickoff, so we sped festively around the stadium, shouting and waving, honking wildly, and raising lumps on pedestrians.

Finally we went into the stadium and wedged ourselves into our seats. I bought Noblesse a balloon. She wrote her phone number on it and released it. Then came the kickoff. Sixty thousand throats shook the earth with their roars. The game was on!

It was one of the most thrilling and colorful afternoons of my life. Although I could not see the field, I knew when I heard cheering that something significant was happening and I yelled as loud as I could. It gave me a sense of belonging. Noblesse joined me, gaily yelling, "I mean block that kick," or "Hold that line, after all."

Between the halves there was a colorful ceremony in which a pick-and-shovel squad marched out into the field in formation and dug up the opposing backfield men whom the Minnesota linemen had driven into the ground. This

77

ceremony had been regularly followed since 1931, when an unseasonal winter thaw had unearthed the body of a Purdue tailback on the 40-yard line where he had lain since the Minnesota-Purdue game the previous fall.

Minnesota won the game 84 to 0. Of course everyone knew Minnesota was going to win. They were just interested in seeing how their jackpot numbers came out.

After the game we met Bob and Peggy outside the stadium. "Let's go over to the Collegiate Eat Shop. Carl Carnage is going to meet us there," said Bob casually.

"Not Carl Carnage, the halfback!" I cried.

"Not his grandmother," said Bob wittily. "He'll be over as soon as he gets paid for today's game."

We went to the restaurant, and Carl Carnage soon joined us. For all his fame and publicity, he was a regular fellow. He let me buy him dinner, and later, when we went to the Golden Grouse, he let me pay for his drinks all night.

The Golden Grouse was a quaint little tavern just outside of Minneapolis that was frequented by the gay college crowd after football games. It was run by two genial Neapolitans, Snake and Trigger Caruso, who had formerly been with Capone. When we arrived the place was already crowded with shouting, singing college people. The waiters scurried energetically about serving the exotic mixed drinks that the college crowd fancied. Behind the bar stood Snake and Trigger Caruso, impassively watering the liquor. The band was playing "Minnesota Rouser."

We joined some friends of Bob's at a large table. "Look at Ed," shrieked a girl at the table, pointing at her escort. "He just drank a zombie, a sloe-gin fizz, a horse's neck, a sidecar, and an old-fashioned—one after the other."

Ed smiled greenly.

A waiter approached. "I'll have a crème de menthe frappé with a beer chaser," said Noblesse. We ordered the same.

We sat around chatting animatedly and drinking. Bob had us in stitches with his imitation of a fat woman putting on her girdle. Carl Carnage talked with a girl at an adjoining table for a while and then took her outside to see an interesting metamorphic rock structure he said he had

noticed up the road a piece. He was studying geology at school.

The other tables, too, were scenes of hilarious abandon. At one a dental student, in an alcoholic display of virtuosity, yanked out his girl's teeth with a pliers. At another a young woman was solemnly putting ice cubes down her escort's back. In the corner a fellow was arguing heatedly with an empty chair.

"I mean I simply adore drinking," Noblesse said to me. "I mean it's so good for my inhibitions."

"Put your dress back on, lady. You'll catch cold," said Snake Caruso, who had come over to the table.

Bob had the place in a panic when he danced with a hall tree. Carl brought his girl in and took another one out. Trigger Caruso restrained a young man who was beating his head against the bar. "But I *like* it," protested the young man. The band kept playing the "Minnesota Rouser."

After we left the Golden Grouse we went to Uncle Tom's Cabin for ribs. Lovable old Uncle Tom saw us coming and hurriedly scribbled doubled prices on the menu. We sang the "Minnesota Rouser," and Bob almost made us split a gut when he insisted on lapping the water in his glass like a dog. By the time we were through eating it was light outside.

Bob stopped in front of the Beta Thigh house, and I took Noblesse to the door. When we reached the door she lifted her face. I kissed her furiously about the chin and mouth. "Tonight will always remain fresh in my heart," I whispered.

She smiled tenderly, and then suddenly the smile disappeared. "The pin!" she exclaimed. "You were supposed to give me the pin today."

I thought frantically of something to say, but it wasn't necessary. All at once her face turned one shade lighter than white, and her eyes rolled up in their sockets. Clapping her hand over her mouth, she bolted into the house.

"Pssst. Yoo, hoo," called Mother Bloor from behind a hedge.

CHAPTER XII

A GREAT DEAL OF NONSENSE has been written about college professors. It has been averred that they live cloistered lives, protected by their ivy-covered, academic walls from the harsh realities of the world. They are supposed to be concerned only with hairsplitting and niceties. They are said to look upon the grimness of our age with loathing.

I know different. Professors are just folks. They are fully as realistic, as informed, and as eager to participate in the affairs of the world as anyone else. I found that out at our Alpha Cholera faculty dinner, a gala annual event to which each member of Alpha Cholera invites a professor.

I wish that the critics of professors could have been there. The conversation at the dinner table alone would have knocked the sheltered-life concept into a cocked hat. So heated were the discussions of burning issues at dinner that one could scarcely get a bite of food into his mouth. Many times I feared they would come to blows over such pertinent arguments as the dates of Pliny, the Elder, the construction of an enthymeme, and the influence of El Greco on Kate Douglas Wiggin.

Nor did the conversation diminish in significance after dinner when we repaired to the library for cigars and coffee substitute. Roger started the phonograph and played a recording of Kolacky's immortal tone poem, "After While, Stella." When the record had stopped Dr. Con Pedale, the learned music professor, said, "The first movement opened with a vigorous theme, sounded by the strings in unison and reinforced alternately by bassoons and horns. Another motive appeared in the wind. The second theme proper was in triple time (3-2) and should have had a more pointed effect, but the corpulence of the first theme made it seem apologetic. The development was dominated by the principal theme. A long pedal announced the recapitulation which was somewhat altered. The scherzo (F major, 1-1 time) presented two themes (the second, of course, in syncopation) and had a trio (6-4 time) with the usual return to the first part thereafter. This composition of Kolacky's ranks in popular favor second only to his immortal concerto, 'Cow Cow Blues.'

"The world came near not ever hearing Kolacky's music. As a boy in Lead, South Dakota, by his own admission, he was not in the least musical. He was chiefly interested in politics. At the age of eleven he ran for park commissioner of Lead but was defeated by Gerhard Schlomm, the incumbent.

"Many years later he acquired a metronome in lieu of a 'Smear' debt owed him by Seth Pestel, a local apothecary. Soon thereafter he was confined to his bed by a severe attack of the glanders. To while away the long days of his illness he picked out simple tunes on his metronome. By the time his doctor pronounced him well again he had already completed his beloved 'Egg Candler Suite.'

"This suite so delighted the governor of South Dakota, Solon Lafferty, that he arranged a pension for Kolacky. Freed of financial worries, Kolacky devoted all his time to composing. During this period he produced his greatest works, among them 'I'm Coming, Thuringia,' and 'Knock 'Em Down, McCluskey.'

"Kolacky's fortune, however, soon came to an end. In the next state election Governor Lafferty was defeated in a Free Soil landslide. The new governor, a tone-deaf man named Harris or Benuti, revoked Kolacky's pension. With his meager savings Kolacky purchased a poultry farm, and there lived out the rest of his life, producing only one composition of any significance, 'The Capons Go Rolling Along.' "

"I shall never forget the night I first heard 'After While, Stella, '" said Dr. Albion Angleterre, a professor of English and quite an authority on England, having spent two weeks there once. "It was while I was in merrie old England. After the concert I went to a funny little place called the Truss and Garter to have a pint of good old stout. I was standing at the bar drinking when I noticed some men throwing darts at a target on the wall. I called over the publican, a fine old British type with a fierce mustache and a face as red as the good beef that nourished him. 'What are they playing, my good man?' I asked.

"'Mind your business or I am out of here,' he replied."

"Speaking of music," said Dr. Sam Cromagnon, a noted professor of anthropology, "I've done some fascinating research on the so-called jungle telegraph, the system of sending messages through the jungle on drums. It's a great deal more complicated than one would think. The drums, for instance, in order to be effective, must be made from the hollow trunks of one special kind of tree —the chrata. No other kind will serve as well. It is no small task to obtain a chrata sufficiently mature to make into a drum. You see, the chrata grows in central Africa, right in the heart of the rain belt, and rain, strangely enough, kills the chrata tree. Consequently, an organization of natives called Chratniks, or friends of the chrata tree, goes about the jungle putting umbrellas on the fledgling chratas.

"And even after the drum is made the difficulties are not at an end. It takes years to train a good drum beater, so intricate is the art. Also, receiving drum messages is no easy matter, for there are only six words in the whole dialect of the region.

"Let me give you some examples. 'Kudu comes on little cat feet' means 'It looks like rain. Haul in your wash.'

"'Cat comes on little kudu feet' means 'All clear. Hang it out again.'

"'Feet comes on little kudu cat' means 'Look primitive, kids. Here comes Osa Johnson.'

"'Little comes on kudu cat feet' means 'Maybe you better leave the wash inside after all. You can't tell about this damn African weather.'"

"Speaking of music," said Dr. Angleterre, "when I was in jolly old England I visited the Chinese-quarter of London, a district called Soho. I was walking down one of the funny little streets that make dear old London the picturesque place that it is. Suddenly I heard a weird wailing note coming out of one of the funny little buildings along the street. It sounded like some sort of reed instrument, although I couldn't figure out which kind. A booby, as London policemen are called, happened to be passing by. I stopped him. 'My good man,' I said, 'what sort of instrument is that playing?'

" 'Why, lord love a duck, gov'nor,' he replied. 'That's no instrument. That's Wang Pu's wife crying.'

" 'Good heavens,' I cried. 'Is he beating her?'

" 'Bless you, no sir,' he said. 'It's just that he's a reactionary, and he won't let her eat with a fork. He says she got to eat with chopsticks, he does. And she can't handle 'em since she lost three fingers last month when she got caught in a fast riffle during a fan-tan game, she did. Poor woman near starves to death. Can't eat nothing with chopsticks except what sticks to 'em, she can't.' "

"It does beat all how a fellow gets set in his ways," said Dr. Frank Newsprint, the eminent professor of journalism. "I remember an A.P man named H. V. Stillborn, a real old-timer who always held the receiver of a telephone between his ear and his shoulder when he talked. He thought French phones were for sissies and would have rather died than used one.

"Well, sir, once he was on a vacation at French Lick Springs. The hotel he was at burned down one night. Everyone in it was killed but Stillborn. Not a newspaperman for hundreds of miles around knew anything about it, it happened so quickly. Stillborn had a clear-cut scoop.

"He rushed out to phone his story to the A.P. But he couldn't find anything but French phones in the whole town of French Lick Springs. He had to walk clear to Muncie before he found an old-style phone and called his office.

"But the phone was in bad order. Stillborn's voice was unclear when it came through to the A.P. office. The rewrite man thought he said *Hot* Springs had had the fire. He flashed the erroneous story all over the country.

"Naturally the Hot Springs Chamber of Commerce took action. They sued the A.P. for $1,000,000, charging that the story had ruined tourist business to that extent. They won the suit, too, but in the appeal the A.P. brought out that the attorney for the Chamber of Commerce, one Lex Legis, did not have a diploma, and the decision was reversed."

"Speaking of newspapers and writing and the like," said Dr. Angleterre, "when I was in dear old England I managed to acquire a very valuable document." He paused for emphasis. "An original Robert Browning manuscript!"

"Which one?" someone asked.

"Well," said Dr. Angleterre, "you can't tell. It seems that Browning's cat spilled a bottle of ink on it, and the whole thing is just a blot. But, you must agree, an original Browning manuscript is an original Browning manuscript."

"My goodness," said Dr. Cromagnon, "look at the time. I must be getting home. I'm preparing a surprise test to spring on my class tomorrow morning. Flunked the whole bunch of them last time I did that," he chuckled.

"By George," said Dr. Newsprint, "I think I'll do that tomorrow too."

"Let's all do it!" cried Dr. Angleterre gaily.

They rose from their chairs, straightened their ties while using the backs of each other's suits for mirrors, put on their hats and coats, and made their good-bys, leaving behind them the not-to-be-soon-forgotten memory of an inspiring evening.

CHAPTER XIII

Les singes sont drolls.—MALRAUX

THE RAINS CAME and wetted down the yellowing
grass. The sky was mottled with teal and mallard flying
south in echelon. The leaves turned yellow, red, brown,
and fluttered crazily to earth. A rogue wind screamed
across the campus scattering broadcast the neat piles of
leaves awaiting their pungent cremation. Now in the mornings the hoar-frost melted grudgingly under a paler sun.
Presently the first snow fell.

Winter had come, and I had not yet made a decision.
Noblesse or Yetta? Noblesse—serene, sophisticated, patrician—the belonger. Yetta—fiery, compassionate, elemental—the crusader. Which? I cursed myself for a
weakling, but I could not decide. I even bought another
fraternity pin and gave it to Noblesse.

I took a walk one night to try to think things out. It
was a cold, invigorating night. The snow crunched under
my feet as I made my way across the starlit, white-crowned
campus. Yetta or Noblesse?

I passed the library. Minnesota has one of the finest
libraries in the country. It has more than two million
volumes, out of which nearly three hundred have been
read, the leader being *Millie* by Donald Henderson Clarke.

The first rule of the library is silence, and that rule is
rigidly enforced. In the reading room, if you want to
turn a page, you raise your hand. The attendant sees it
and presses a button which turns on a green light. That
is a signal for everyone in the room to put cotton in their
ears. Then you turn the page.

Noblesse or Yetta?

Now I was in front of the chemistry building. Minnesota has one of the finest chemistry schools in the country. It was, in fact, at Minnesota that the four elements—earth, air, fire, and water—were discovered.

By day the chemistry building is filled with intelligent young men and women holding beakers over Bunsen burners. Bunsen burners differ from ordinary burners in that they do not burn gas, but Bunsen. Some of the students study organic chemistry and some inorganic. As you know, organic chemistry is the study of organs, like the Wurlitzer, the Hammond Electric, and the Novachord. Inorganic chemistry is the study of the insides of organs.

The work of the chemist is to extract gold from the baser metals.

Yetta or Noblesse?

Before me was the medical building. Minnesota has one of the finest medical schools in the country. Thousands of ailing people come here annually for treatment and observation, and many cases are indeed unusual. Not long ago, for instance, a young woman named Copra Wyatt came in and complained of a growth on her back. The examining doctor was unable to determine the nature of the growth. "Let's let it grow for a while and see what it is," he told Miss Wyatt.

She did, and later she was glad that she followed the doctor's advice because it turned out to be a coconut palm, and today she makes a comfortable living selling coconut milk in the foyer of the Stock Exchange in New York.

Noblesse or Yetta?

I passed the law building. Minnesota has one of the finest law schools in the country. Students are not only taught the theory of law, they also spend a great deal of time studying actual cases. Indeed, many of the cases they study are enough to baffle a lawyer of many years' experience, yea, a judge even. I am in mind of the extremely complicated Gothic-Flanders-Nebulous-Bucolic-Tonsure action at law.

To properly understand this case we must go back to 1924. One night in the spring of that year Bernhard Gothic was walking down a country road near Etoile du Nord, Minnesota. He kept in the shadows because he was a fugitive from justice. He was wanted for nepotism in Iowa and Nebraska. Gothic had not eaten that day. He was looking for a chicken coop so that he could steal a chicken and make a pillow with its feathers. He was unable to sleep comfortably on the hard ground at night. He spied a chicken coop and stole in—rather noisily, because he was inept at that sort of thing.

The chickens set up a hue and cry which carried to the farmhouse and was heard by the proprietress of the farm, a widow woman named Moll Flanders. When she heard the commotion she dropped the ouija board with which she had been trying to communicate with her son, Duncan, who had gone to sea and disappeared many years before. Grabbing a flashlight, she ran out to the coop.

Her beam of light fell on the prostrate form of Bernhard Gothic hopelessly entangled in one hundred and twenty feet of chicken wire. Mrs. Flanders screamed when she saw Gothic. He happened to resemble her son Duncan slightly, and she thought it was he come home at last. She fell on Gothic with tears and protestations of affection. He shrewdly kept his big mouth shut.

She took him into the house and fed him. To her numerous questions he answered that he had recently suffered an attack of amnesia and it would take a long period of good nourishment and rest before he was himself again. He wasn't born Tuesday.

Then a well-rounded wench in a wrapper came down from upstairs. "This here's your baby sister Irma," said Mrs. Flanders. "Do you remember her?"

"Oh hell, yes," said Gothic. "Gimme a slobber, sis."

Mrs. Flanders, more alarmed than pleased at the violence of his fraternal affection, finally pried them loose and sent Gothic to bed.

He stayed for several months, eating five copious meals a day and swinging in the hammock between meals. It would have been perfect except for Irma. Her contours slipped disturbingly into all his gastronomic reveries. Finally he could stand the artificial continence of their relationship no longer. He went to her and told her the

whole truth. He wouldn't have if he had known what a big blabbermouth she was.

She ran right to her mother and told her, but Mrs. Flanders only screamed, "Liar! Jezebel!" and hit her in the mouth with a darning egg. Irma packed her chattels and hied herself to St. Paul in a fit of pique.

Mrs. Flanders went to Gothic and said, "Son, you're all I got left now. Promise Ma you'll never leave her."

"Sure, sure," he said.

"Women ain't no good, son," she continued. "Don't you be gettin' married to none of 'em. You stay here with yore pore old ma, and don't take on with no women, and I'll leave you somethin' mighty nice in my will."

"I gotcha," he said.

In St. Paul Irma tried unsuccessfully to find a job for several weeks and finally enrolled in Tom Tonsure's college for lady barbers.

As part of his college Tonsure ran a cut-rate barbershop. When students had completed their basic training they went to work in the shop for a time. Eventually Irma was promoted to the shop.

One day Rex Nebulous, a desk clerk at the Fireproof Hotel in St. Paul, came into Tonsure's shop to get a haircut. Nebulous was almost bald; that is why he patronized this cheap shop. As he said smilingly, "I don't want to pay full price for half a haircut."

He sat in Irma's chair. As Irma cut his sparse hair she noticed a faint inscription on top of his scalp. Bending closer, she read the almost illegible words, "Good-by, Mama—Duncan."

"These words on your head. Where did they come from?" she asked excitedly.

"That happened a long time ago," Nebulous answered. "I was just a little boy then. It was on the *Titanic*. The ship was going down, and there were not enough lifeboats for everyone. I remember a young sailor putting me in the last boat and writing this message on my head. I was bald then too. I guess I never had no hair," he giggled.

"And the sailor. What happened to him?"

"He went down with the ship, poor fellow. I saw him go under."

It *was* Duncan! Now she would show that impostor. Now she had proof. Now she would succor her poor, victimized old mother. She waved her arms joyously, forgetting that she had a razor in her hand. Nebulous' ear dropped gently to the floor.

Fortunately, Tom Tonsure had learned to keep a doctor in constant attendance for just such occurrences. Nebulous' ear was rapidly stitched back on, and, mollified by a free bottle of brilliantine, he left amicably.

Meanwhile, back on the farm Gothic was getting restless. He took long, randy walks around the countryside. During the course of his libidinous constitutionals he chanced on a comely lass named Frances Bucolic up the road a piece. Gothic applied all his amorous arts, and she succumbed.

But not completely. She wanted to get married first. He could not dissuade her. Finally he reached a compromise. He said he would marry her if she kept it a secret from Mrs. Flanders. She grudgingly agreed. They sneaked away one night to a justice of the peace in St. Paul and then took a room at the Fireproof Hotel.

Rex Nebulous was at the desk that night. About 2 A.M. a customer called the desk and informed Nebulous that a dry-goods drummer was enjoying an unsanctified union in Room 415. Nebulous had the phone to his recently severed ear. He thought his informant said Room 450, which was occupied by Bernhard Gothic and his bride. He called in two cops and told them to get up to Room 450. The cops broke down the door, wrapped the newlyweds in a blanket, and hauled them off to jail.

Gothic was quite willing to forget the whole thing, but Frances was outraged. She swore out a complaint against Nebulous, charging him with false arrest.

The unhappy Nebulous blamed all his misfortunes on his damaged ear. He instituted suit for damages against Tom Tonsure.

Tonsure filed suit against Irma, charging criminal negligence.

Irma swore out a complaint against Gothic, charging him with fraud.

Mrs. Flanders, when she heard of it, did not believe

that her "son" was married. She thought he was the victim of a blackmail plot by Frances Bucolic. She charged Frances with extortion and fornication. She further swore out a complaint against Irma, charging her with stealing four spoons when she left home.

Frances filed a counter-charge of defamation against Mrs. Flanders.

The distraught St. Paul police threw them all in jail while they tried to clarify the issues of the case. They stayed in jail for months as more and more arguments were heard, and the case got more and more confused.

They might be there to this day had it not been for one peculiar circumstance. The custodian of the St. Paul jail, one Yale Towne, was engaged in a shady deal with a certain Sam Provendor, a grocer. Provendor had a contract to provide the jail with groceries. He was paid for good quality food, but instead he delivered the cheapest kind of substandard merchandise and split the profits with Towne.

During the course of this ramified case Provendor delivered a supply of condemned salmon to the jail. It was given to the principals for dinner. After they had eaten, they all complained of feeling poorly and went to bed. During the night every one of them quietly passed away.

The police were so grateful to Provendor for relieving them of this muddle that they did not prosecute. In fact, they gave him a police card that let him through fire lines. As a gesture of appreciation Provendor throws a picnic for the force at Phalen Park in St. Paul every summer.

Yetta or Noblesse?

I passed the engineering building. Minnesota has one of the finest engineering schools in the country. It is filled with excellent modern equipment gyrocompos and catapults, and catalysts, and catacombs, and what not. Minnesota once came within an ace of having an atom smasher too.

That was a few years back. Carl Cantilever, an engineering professor, designed an atom smasher that would cost $1,000,000 to build. He asked for the money from the Board of Regents of the University which passes on all appropriations. Since Cantilever wanted such a large sum, they called a special meeting and asked him to attend.

All the Regents sat and listened while Cantilever explained the function of the proposed atom smasher—that is, all except Phineas Topsoil, who was out looking at some bottom land and said he would get there as soon as he could. Cantilever finished his explanation and asked if there were any questions.

"After you get the atom in the machine," said one Regent, "can you see it?"

"No," said Cantilever.

"Can you hear it?" asked another.

"No," said Cantilever.

"Can you smell it?" asked a third.

"No," said Cantilever.

"Well," they chorused, "then how do you know it's there?"

Cantilever rubbed his chin and smiled. "Gentlemen," he said, "have you ever had a toothache?"

They nodded.

"Could you see it?"

"No," they said.

"Could you hear it?"

"No," they said.

"Could you smell it?"

"No," they said.

Cantilever spread out his hands. "Well, then, how do you know you had it?"

Well, sir, he certainly had them there.

Then Phineas Topsoil walked in.

"We're going to give this here man a appropriation of $1,000,000 for to build a atom smasher," the Regents said to Topsoil.

"What's a atom smasher?" asked Topsoil.

Cantilever patiently explained all over again.

When he had finished Topsoil asked, "After you get the atom in the machine, can you see it?"

"No," said Cantilever.

"Can you hear it?"

"No," said Cantilever.

"Can you smell it?"

"No," said Cantilever.

"Well, then, how do you know it's there?"

Cantilever rubbed his chin and smiled. "Mr. Topsoil," he said, "have you ever had a toothache?"

The Regents winked and nudged each other.

"No," said Topsoil.

Cantilever frowned. "Never had a toothache?"

"No."

"Not even a little one?"

"No."

"Maybe a long time ago?"

"No."

"That's hard to understand," said Cantilever.

"No, 'tain't," gummed Topsoil. "No teeth. No appropriation."

Noblesse or Yetta?

I was in front of the music building. Minnesota has one of the finest music schools in the country. Students are given every encouragement to become accomplished musicians, and achievement is well rewarded. Every year the top students in the school give a public recital, which is indeed a gala musical event.

At a recital some time ago there was a rather interesting occurrence. A Miss Grace Barren was piano soloist for the evening. She was to play two numbers. De Falla's "Ritual Fire Dance" was the first. At the conclusion of this number Miss Barren rose to take a bow in acknowledgment of the thunderous applause. She did not know that her dress had become entangled in the thread of the music stool.

As she leaned over to bow there was a rip and she stood on the stage divested. Her deepest secret was revealed to the world. She wore false pectorals.

But Miss Barren was a trouper. Back to the piano she went and played her second number. It was Bach's "Two-Part Invention."

Yetta or Noblesse?

Yetta, the proletarian. Noblesse, the patrician. All through the fall I had taken out first one, then the other. To both I had confessed my love. To both I had given my Alpha Cholera pin. Now this vacillation must cease. Was I a man or a shuttlecock?

I stopped by a stately oak (Minnesota has some of the finest oaks in the country) and removed a coin from my pocket. Let the impersonal gods of chance be my arbiters, for a decision must be reached.

My thumb flexed under the coin ready to flip it on its fateful spin. I closed my eyes for a moment. Then, as if a being apart from me, my thumb snapped up.

The coin flew into the air. Languidly, it seemed, it turned over and over and over as it ascended. Suddenly it plummeted downward, my destiny in its inscrutable, minted features.

CHAPTER XIV

Il sait jouer du piano.—DE GAULLE

THE COIN FELL in a snowbank.

I got down on my knees and began to shovel rapidly with my hands. Deeper and deeper I dug, but the elusive coin was nowhere to be seen. Suddenly I heard footsteps in the snow behind me. I looked up. It was Mr. Ingelbretsvold, the freshman adviser.

"Good evening, Mr. Ingelbretsvold," I said, rising to my feet.

"Why, it's Ira Hearthrug," he said.

"Asa," I corrected.

"That's what I meant," he said. "Well, well, out taking a little air, I see. It certainly is fine weather. This early snow will certainly help the farmers."

"Yes," I said. "It should freeze every pumpkin in Minnesota."

"That's what I meant," he said. "Freeze those damn pumpkins. Altogether too many people going around scaring people with those damn jack-o'-lanterns. But enough of this agricultural chitchat. Are you walking this way?"

"No," I said.

"Good. We'll walk together. I have to meet a lady down here a little way. Tell me," he said as we walked, "how are you getting along in school?"

"Fine," I said.

"You're following the program I made out for you?"

"Yes."

"And you're learning a great deal?"

"A little of everything."

96

"Fine," he said. "That's what college is for—to make you a well-rounded-out personality. You've got to know a little of everything. You can never tell when somebody is going to come up to you on the street and ask you if monkshood is ranunculaceous or how many pence there are in a groat. College should prepare you for those things. If there's anything I hate it's somebody who is going to college to learn how to *do* something. Why don't they go go to a trade school if they want to learn how to *do* something? *Do* something, *do* something, *do* something —it makes me so damn mad!" he screamed furiously, slashing me across the face with his alpenstock.

"*Do* something," he continued in a milder tone. "What's the use of knowing how to *do* something if your personality is not well rounded out, huh? I tell you, colleges aren't what they used to be. When I was a boy there were no schools of medicine or law or engineering in a university. There was an arts college, and when you finished, you didn't know how to *do* anything. No sir. But, by God, you were a well-rounded-out personality. Now, every year, I see more and more students going into the professional colleges and the technical colleges, and I can see that the day of gentlemen in a university is drawing to a close. Sometimes I feel like giving it all up."

"Take heart, Mr. Ingelbretsvold," I cried, "for there are still those of us who know what a university is for."

"Yes, you're right," he said. "I spoke hastily. There'll always be some who don't want to *do* anything. The arts college, sir, will survive. But tell me about yourself. How else, besides classes, are you rounding out your personality? Are you reading?"

"Yes. I just finished a mystery by Chrisgitha Aggie. It's called *The Case of the Hernious Hostler*. It's about the disappearance of a prime minister. He is scheduled to make a vitally important speech at noon. At fifteen minutes before noon he is seen by many people, but at noon he has disappeared from the face of the earth. The leader of the opposition party rises and says that the prime minister has deserted his country and that the people should revolt. Well, they are all set to follow the advice of the opposition leader when at twenty minutes past twelve the prime minister drops from the sky. It seems that he had been walking in the roof garden of the parliament house meditating before his momentous speech. In his preoccupation he had slipped and fallen off the roof. Luckily the minute hand of the clock on the wall of the parliament house had caught in his trousers and prevented him from crashing to earth. The minute hand at this time pointed to fourteen minutes to twelve. It was not until the hand swung to twenty past twelve that gravity allowed the prime minister to continue his fall."

"I see," said Mr. Ingelbretsvold. "How about extra-curricular activities? Are you active in them?"

"I'm an Alpha Cholera," I said proudly.

"Fine. Splendid. And"—he prodded me slyly in the ribs—"how about the fair sex?"

"More than I can handle," I said modestly. "Twice as much."

"Excellent, my boy. You'll soon be a well-rounded-out personality." He stopped walking. Across the street a woman stood under a lamppost. "Well, this is as far as I go," said Mr. Ingelbretsvold. "There's my party across the street. Stop in and see me if there's anything I can do for you. Good night."

He walked across the street, and took the woman's arm. It was Mother Bloor.

As I walked slowly home Mr. Ingelbretsvold's words kept running through my head. "A well-rounded-out personality." That's what college should make you. You must learn a little of everything. Everything. Suddenly my problem was solved.

I did not have to choose between Noblesse and Yetta; I did not have to give up either of them. Yetta and Noblesse represented the opposite poles of collegiate life. What better way to learn a little of everything than by going with both of them? What better way to round out my personality?

My step was quicker now, and I was whistling. I decided not to go back to the snowbank and look for that coin. I would undoubtedly find it during the January thaw.

CHAPTER XV

Monsieur, les autres personnes qui habitent cet hôtel protestent contre ce bruit insupportable.
—LOUIS XIV

ON MONDAY NIGHTS the Alpha Cholera actives held their chapter meetings. I used to sit outside the door of the chapter room, feeling lonely and left out, hoping to overhear something of the momentous business that was going on inside, for I was but a pledge and I could not go in. But now spring had come, and I had become an active. Now truly I was a part of Alpha Cholera, a performer of its functions, a shaper of its destiny. I could go to chapter meetings.

I'll confess that I was nervous at my first chapter meeting and that I had doubts about my ability to fulfill all my new responsibilities. But everyone was so kind and reassuring that I was soon confidently at ease. After we sang the Alpha Cholera hymn Roger opened the meeting. "For the benefit of the new actives," he said with a kindly glance at me, "I will explain the procedure of the chapter meetings. In these meetings we take care of the routine business of running a fraternity—dances, parties, financial matters, and so forth. But what is perhaps more important, we make and consider suggestions on how to improve our fraternity, how to make it even better than it is. Oh, of course we know that we have the best fraternity at the University now, but just the same—and I want to impress this on the new actives—a fraternity that is not constantly progressing is a fraternity that is moving backwards.

"One of the best ways to improve a fraternity is to im-

100

prove each individual member, for, after all, what is a fraternity but a group of members, huh? To improve the individual members, at the beginning of each chapter meeting we have what we call a 'friendly criticism period.' During this period we give friendly criticisms and helpful hints to any members who have not been conducting themselves in a manner that reflects credit on Alpha Cholera. These criticisms are made and accepted in the spirit of good fellowship and for the good of all.

"All right, let's get started with the 'friendly criticism period.' "

An active stood up. "I want to say a few words to Asa," he said. "I am going to say these things because I know we are all friends here and we are all interested in the welfare of Alpha Cholera. I have been noticing Asa's clothes, and I do not think they reflect credit on the fraternity. In the first place, he wears pants, coat, and vest from the same suit. As we all know, this is not being done. Your coat must never match your pants, and vests are not being worn unless they do not match either coat or pants. Furthermore, pants must be pegged to fit snugly around the ankle, and coats should extend to the midpoint of the femur except on festive occasions, when knee length is permissible.

"Now, to discuss haberdashery. I notice that Asa's shirts do not have button-down collars. Well, one might as well wear no shirt at all. As for neckwear, I should like to point out that only dark red, knit wool ties are *à la mode* —unless, of course, one is going to a funeral or public execution, where black knit wools are proper." He sat down.

Another rose. "I want to add a few words about Asa," he said. "What I have to say is in the spirit of the greatest friendship and for the good of the fraternity. It has been reported to me, and I have seen it myself, that Asa has been observed riding in a convertible in which the top was *up,* the seats were not filled, and nobody was yelling. I want to say, in a friendly way, naturally, that it's things like that that can give a fraternity a bad name. When riding in a convertible the top must always be *down,* no matter what the weather, and there must never be fewer than eight people in the convertible, and they must all be yelling."

As soon as he sat down another stood up. "I have a few suggestions to make to Asa in the spirit of friendship and for the benefit of Alpha Cholera. As you know, people are not judged so much on what they say as on how they say it. Consequently, I think we must all be careful with our diction. I have heard Asa, when speaking of music, call phonograph records 'phonograph records.' Nobody in the know says that. Phonograph records are called 'discs' or 'platters.' And one doesn't 'turn a record over and play the other side.' One 'flips and spins the plattermate.'

"Also, I have heard Asa say that he was going to 'hear a Negro band.' No. One 'digs the colored men.' "

Another active continued the discussion. "While on the subject of diction," he said, "I want to make a friendly criticism for the good of the fraternity about Asa's speech. Asa says 'on *the* campus.' That is incorrect. One says simply 'on campus.' And the plural of campus is 'campi.' "

"Yes," put in another. "Asa must learn the proper diction concerning women. I make this criticism in a friendly spirit and for the good of the fraternity. I have heard Asa describe a pretty girl as 'pretty' and an ugly girl as 'ugly.' A pretty girl is described with a leer as a 'smooth operator.' If the girl is extremely pretty it is correct to drool. An ugly girl is described as 'not what you would call a beauty, but a awful swell kid, loads of fun, lot of personality, lot of drive.' "

There did not seem to be any more, so I stood up. "I want to thank my brother members for their kind interest in me and for their helpful suggestions. Now I would like to say a few words in the spirit of friendship and for the good of the fraternity."

"We will now proceed to the business part of the meeting," Roger interrupted.

Eino Ffliiikkiinnenn, the sergeant at arms, hit me in the mouth. "You outa order," he growled.

Roger continued: "We have received a request for one

dollar from the Crippled Children's Hospital. Is there any discussion?"

"I'd like to say something," said Shylock Fiscal, our treasurer.

"Go ahead, Shy," said Roger.

"Thanks, Rog," said Shy. "Now, nobody likes crippled children better than I do. I'm simply mad about them. But I don't think we should be too hasty about granting this request. A dollar here, a dollar there, it mounts up. In these times, like Daddy says, with a bunch of visionaries and radicals in Washington, you never know where you're going to be tomorrow. I say charity begins at home. I move that we refuse this request."

"Motion carried," said Roger. "Now we'll have a discussion about our spring formal which is going to be held in another six weeks. I'm going to call on Shy, who has been working very hard as arrangements chairman, to give his report."

"Thanks, Rog. Yes, I have been working pretty hard, even if I do say so myself," he chuckled. "But I want to tell you that there's no greater satisfaction in the world than working hard—*and* accomplishing something—for your fraternity. Yes sir.

"Well, first there was the matter of hiring a band. I sent letters to every name band in the country, asking for bids on our dance. They all sent back answers except Jimmy Dorsey, who sent back an autographed picture. I guess he misunderstood my letter. The lowest bid was from Artie Shaw. He wants $10,000, which is not unreasonable, except that he can't be *here* to play. He has an engagement in Chicago, but he says he can arrange to have his music broadcast up here to our dance.

"Well, I looked over the bids and I looked them over, and finally I decided that there was only one thing to do: I had to go look for a band myself. So I just dropped everything and hit for New York.

"The trip cost $1,000, but that's nothing compared to what I saved you kids. I found a band, and what a band. The name of it is Sax Coburg and His Tooters. We haven't heard much of them out here in the Midwest, but I want to tell you they've made quite a name for themselves playing the more *intime* supper clubs in Brooklyn and Elizabeth, New Jersey. It's a three-piece combination—drums, accordion, and banjo. And you won't believe this, but I got them for only $3,000.

"Of course they can't play all night. They have to quit at nine-thirty to catch a train for an engagement at the Benton Harbor, Michigan, grape festival. But they're going to leave us a stack of their home recordings, and we can play them all we want on our phonograph. They said we could keep the records.

"Now about the place for the dance. You can't have a dance without you have a place to have it, can you? Heh, heh, heh. Well, if you remember we held our dance in the gymnasium of Central High School last year, and that didn't go over at all. Through some error a basketball game had been scheduled for the same night between Central and Hrdlicka Prep. Well, it wasn't much fun dancing with kids dribbling all around the floor, and throwing body checks into you, and dropping the ball in the punch bowl. Central finally won the game, 32 to 31 in an overtime period.

"I resolved that nothing was going to mar our dance this year. I got a place to hold our dance that's going to be the talk of the campus for many months to come. I rented a houseboat! Yes, I did. And what's more, I rented a motor launch to tow us twenty miles down the river and back while we danced. The payoff is that by talking fast and using the old bean I got the whole business for $1,500."

"Well," said Roger, "I certainly think we owe Shylock a debt of gratitude for the way he handled the arrangements."

"There's a couple more things, Rog," said Shylock.

"Oh, excuse me. Go ahead, Shy," said Roger.

"Thanks, Rog. Now about corsages. Every spring formal in the past all us fellows have been spending a lot of money for orchids and roses and whatnot, and we know that by the middle of the evening the corsages were always wilted and looked like something the cat dragged in. Well, that isn't going to happen this year. No sir.

"I've made a deal—I mean I made a deal for *you*—with the Apex Novelty Company. They are going to supply us with artificial orchids. Believe me, I've seen them, and it's impossible to tell them from the real article. They're even artificially perfumed. They smell *better* than orchids. And they positively will not wilt. They're going to cost us $10 apiece, which is ridiculously low, everything considered.

"And now, last, but certainly not least—heh, heh, heh —let's discuss the tickets for the formal. We know that we're going to have the best Alpha Cholera dance ever, and we know, too, that it's going to cost quite a little money, more than we have in our treasury. Of course it's worth every cent of it. Yes sir. You can't buy the time we're going to have for twice the money. And I know that it's getting toward the end of the year and you fellows are a little short right now. So I'll tell you what I'm going to do. I'm going to sell you your tickets for $30 apiece, and if there's any deficit I'll make it up out of my own pocket."

"As president of Alpha Cholera," said Roger, "I want to extend the appreciation of its members to you, Shy. Although you haven't received any tangible reward for your unselfish labors, I assure you that the thanks of Alpha Cholera are yours."

"That's reward enough for me," said Shylock huskily.

I brushed aside a tear.

"After all Shy has done for us," said Roger, "I want to see a 100 per cent turnout at the formal. Anybody who doesn't buy tickets will get fined $100 and get his butter privileges permanently revoked.

"Now, is there any new business?"

"Yah," said Eino Ffiliikkiinnennn, putting down the dead mouse he was stroking. "Ay going to qvit."

"Quit Alpha Cholera!" cried Roger. "Surely you jest."

"No. Ay qvit. Ay going to yoin Mu Beta Fistula."

"Are they going to pay you more than we do, Eino?"

"No."

"We'll give you more money."

"No. Ay qvit."

"But why, Eino? Don't we treat you well?"

"Yes, bot Ay qvit."

"What's the reason? Are they giving you something that we don't have?"

"Yes. Dey going to give me nice lady to tell me stories before I go to bed," said Eino, and was gone.

"That's a fine how-do-you-do," complained Roger. "Imagine him walking out like that. After all we've done for him—buying him a pony, putting a soda fountain in his room, wiping his nose for him—Oh, what's the use of talking?"

"That sure leaves Alpha Cholera in a fine spot," said Shylock. "We haven't got a single B.M.O.C. in the fraternity now. How are we ever going to get anybody to pledge next year? We did bad enough this year," he added with a nod at me.

"That's right," said Roger sadly. "No football players, no basketball players, not even a baseball player. We haven't even got anybody in campus politics. If we only had somebody who held some kind of office."

"There's a campus election in a few weeks," Shylock suggested.

"Yes," Roger answered, "but they're only electing a bunch of small-time offices—Keep Your Campus Clean Committees, Less Starchy Foods for Lunch Committee, Committee to Acquaint Students with the Words of 'Minnesota Rouser'—nothing that would make a B.M.O.C."

"How about the freshman representative to the student council? That's important enough to make a B.M.O.C.," said Shylock.

"But what good does that do us?" asked Roger. "We haven't got any smooth freshman."

"There's Asa," suggested Shylock.

Roger laughed. "This is no time for jokes."

"I'm serious," said Shylock.

"But *Asa!*" protested Roger.

"He's the only freshman we've got."

Roger thought for a few minutes. "Should we try it?"

"What the hell," said Shylock.

"Asa," said Roger, "come up here." I came to the chair. "We've watched you since you've joined Alpha Cholera with a great deal of pride and satisfaction. We've helped

WANTED FOR NEPOTISM

you along whenever we could. We've done all in our power for you. We've tried to make you an Alpha Cholera."

"I know! I know!" I exclaimed.

"Yes," said Shylock. "To us you've somehow been more than just another pledge. Maybe it's because we knew you had the old moxie, the old get out and get. And now we think you're ready, ready to be tried."

"Asa," said Roger softly, "we want you to run for freshman representative to the student council."

I blanched. Roger blanched. Shylock blanched. We blanched all three. "But who would vote for me?" I cried.

"That is a problem," said Roger.

"Just leave that to us," said Shylock. "All you have to do now is file for the office, smile at everybody you see, and give away all the cigarettes you can."

"The meeting is now adjourned," said Roger. "Instead of our usual song to close the meeting we will kneel in silent prayer for sixty seconds."

CHAPTER XVI

Quelle heure est-il?—FLAUBERT

"ASA," said Roger, "this is Rudy Caucus, the president of the Yahoo party."

"How do you do?" I said.

"He ain't much to look at," said Rudy.

"Oh, I don't know," said Shylock. "He's got a good carriage."

"Look at his fine head," added Roger.

"I've seen better heads on beers," said Rudy.

I smiled modestly.

"Besides," Rudy continued, "nobody ever heard of him."

"That's just the point," said Roger. "You need an unknown to win this election."

"He's a dark horse," said Shylock.

I whinnied modestly.

"Look at the Mafia candidate," Shylock went on. "Petey Loadsafun, the smoothest freshman on campus. You couldn't possibly get a candidate half as smooth as Loadsafun. That's out. The only sharp thing to do is to run an unknown, a dark horse."

"Asa's a dark horse," said Roger.

"So was Landon," said Rudy.

"Yes, but so was Franklin Pierce," Roger said.

"Who was Franklin Pierce?" asked Rudy.

" 'Who was Franklin Pierce?' he says," said Shylock. "Just the President of the United States, that's all."

"And he was a dark horse," Roger said.

"I never heard of him," Rudy said. "When was he President?"

"Did you ever hear of Black Friday?" asked Shylock.

"No," said Rudy.

"Black Friday occurred during the administration of Franklin Pierce," Shylock explained. "Black Friday was so called because of a total eclipse of the sun which took place on that day. Taking advantage of the darkness, Jay Gould, a financier, walked into the vault of the subtreasury in New York, told a bemused guard that he was Grover Whalen, then secretary of the treasury, and made off with all the gold in the country.

"When the gold was discovered missing, the entire financial structure of the nation threatened to collapse. Jay Gould notified the President, Franklin Pierce——"

"The dark horse," Roger put in.

"——that he had the gold, but he wouldn't give it back unless Thomas Nasty, political cartoonist on the New York *Domestick Intelligencer,* quit drawing funny pictures of Doss Tweed who was betrothed to Gould's daughter Eileen or Irene. Nasty replied, 'I'm d-mned if I will.'

"It looked pretty black for a while, but at the last minute Franklin Pierce appealed to Nasty's wife, an eczemic harridan named Birdie, to intercede for the benefit of the country. Birdie persuaded Nasty to quit his job on the *Domestick Intelligencer* and go to work as weighmaster at the Reading Coal and Dock Company. Nasty consented, but proclaimed that he had *not* been intimidated and that he was taking the new job merely to be nearer his family in Wilkes-Barre. He said that he had not heard from his family in several years because his mother, a religious fanatic, would not allow a telephone in the house.

"Gould, true to his word, gave all the gold back save one bar of bullion which he had fashioned into a soap dish and which can still be seen at the Gould mansion in Plentywood, Montana. The country was saved."

"And you say this Pierce was a dark horse?" asked Rudy.

"Like Asa," said Roger.

Rudy considered for a moment. "All right, I'll take a chance."

"You'll never regret it," said Shylock. "Now let's figure out a campaign for Asa."

"That's easy," said Roger. "The Mafia has been in power for three years. We'll charge them with malfeasance."

"I thought of that," said Rudy. "But you can't. They never did anything."

"What do you mean?" asked Roger. "They've controlled the student council for three years. They must have done something."

"No," said Rudy. "They were careful. They never took any action. Whenever something came up they always *passed a resolution* to take action. They never *took* action."

"How astute," said Shylock.

"Yes," agreed Rudy.

"Well, let's introduce a new issue then," Roger suggested.

"How about lowering tuition?" asked Shylock.

"No good," Rudy answered. "It would make the election too popular. The whole student body would get out and vote. We wouldn't be able to control the election. It's getting hard enough to handle the fraternity and sorority votes without letting every Tom, Dick, and Harry in on the election. We want an issue that won't attract too much attention, something controversial, but of no concern to the barbs."

"That's right," Shylock said. "Well, is there anything in the Mafia party platform that we could make an issue of?"

"I don't think so," said Rudy. "It is by way of being the most innocuous political document of our time. We're dealing with a shrewd adversary."

"Have you got a copy? Let's take a look at it. Maybe we can find something," said Roger.

"All right. I'll read it," Rudy said. "'The Mafia party,'" he read, "'with the straightforwardness that has carried it to victory in the last three years and with a firm conviction of the intelligence of the student voters which has been conclusively demonstrated in the last three years, announces its program and aims in this election.

"'1. We believe that except for saddle shoes, white

shoes should not be worn on campus before Memorial Day and after Labor Day.' "

"You can't quarrel with that," Shylock admitted.

" '2. We believe that students should help blind men across streets unless the students themselves are blind."

"That's sound enough," said Roger.

" '3. We believe that the last student to leave a classroom, in the interests of economy and conservation of the resources of our beloved country, the United States of America, should turn out the lights, unless there is someone remaining in the room."

"Nothing wrong with that," Shylock said.

" '4. We believe that when visiting sick patients in hospitals students should bring along candy, fruit, or flowers whenever possible.' "

"That sounds all right," said Roger.

" '5. We believe that in case of fire in one or more campus buildings students should proceed in an orderly manner to the nearest exit, unless there is one closer.' "

"No argument there," Shylock said.

" '6. We believe that male students should remove their hats in elevators when there are ladies present.' "

"You can't make an issue of that," said Roger.

"Wait a minute," Shylock cried. "That's it. There's our issue. Listen, the Mafia says flatly that a fellow should take his hat off when there are women in an elevator. Well, what if the elevator is real crowded, jam packed? Say there's a fellow in there with his hat on. A woman comes in. She's loaded down with packages. She just barely manages to squeeze into the elevator. Now, if this fellow takes off his hat it means that he is going to have to hold it in front of him. All right. In order to hold his hat in front of him, he's got to hold his arm straight out from the elbow. See what I mean? He's taking up twice as much room as he did when the hat was on his head! All right. Remember the elevator was jammed. This fellow was standing with his hands pinned down at his sides, unable to move, when the woman came in. Now he has to take his hat off and hold it. He can't hold it on either side; he has to hold it in front of him. Now then, who is in front of him? The woman, of course. So he takes off his hat, puts it in his hand, sticks out his arm, jabs the woman in the back, knocks her packages out of her hand, shoves her into the elevator doors, and causes her to suffer severe physical injury and perhaps trauma. That's what the Mafia wants you to do."

"Shy, you're a genius!" exclaimed Roger.

Shylock smiled modestly. "I try my best," he said simply.

"I think that's going to be all right," Rudy said. "It's a brand-new issue. Maybe we'll catch Mafia off their guard."

Roger and Shylock shook hands.

"Yes," said Rudy. "I like that. It's controversial enough to provide a little action during the campaign and insipid enough to keep the riffraff from voting."

"You know," mused Roger, "it's a wonder they don't put up a candidate of their own. They've got the votes to elect anybody they want."

"No organization," said Rudy. "Numbers aren't enough. You got to have organization. We and the Mafia are the only campus parties that amount to anything, and that's because we've got organization. Oh, of course the Subversive Elements League always runs somebody, but we don't even count their ballots. Then there's the independent candidates, but they're usually kids majoring in elocution who use the election to practice their lessons. We've got nothing to worry about from the barbs.

"Besides, they don't even want to have anything to do with campus politics. I've talked to them, and I know. Just the other day I met a kid and asked him if he was going to vote. 'Nah,' he said. 'What for?'

" 'Don't you care who runs your student government?' I asked.

" 'Nah,' he said. 'They don't govern. They just hold meetings. What do I care who holds meetings?'

" 'What school are you in?' I asked him.

" 'Medicine,' he said.

" 'I see. And what are you getting out of the University?'

" 'I'm learning to be a doctor,' he said. 'And when I graduate I'll go out and heal the sick.'

" 'Then he said to me, 'Are you going to vote?'

" 'I'm the president of the Yahoo party,' I answered with becoming modesty.

" 'What do you get out of it?' he asked.

" 'Well,' I said, 'I'm making contacts and learning how to deal with people and discovering my own character.'

" 'I see,' he said. 'What school are you in?'

" 'I'm in liberal arts.'

" 'How are your grades?' he asked.

"I drew myself up. 'I'm not concerned with the obsolete practice of giving grades. To me rounding out my personality is more important than any meaningless alphabetical symbols.'

" 'What are you going to do after you graduate?" he asked.

" 'I'm not worried about that unlikely event,' I answered. 'The kind of education I'm getting will equip me for anything that might come up.' "

"I guess you told him," said Roger.

"Yes," Rudy admitted. "I tell you, those people don't deserve to vote. They haven't got the proper spirit. Why, they don't even know what the University is for."

"Yup," agreed Shylock. "Well, I guess we're all set to get going on the campaign."

"Yeah," said Rudy. "Get hold of the Minnesota *Daily* political reporter and give him a statement. His name is Dacmon Scoop. Give him some kind of a story every day. He's a good kid. He'll give you plenty of publicity. He gets paid on space rates. That's about all you can do during the campaign.

"Don't worry too much about the campaign. It doesn't mean much. The important work comes the day before the election. On that day you call all the sororities and fraternities that have candidates running in this election and tell each one of them that you will guarantee the entire Alpha Cholera vote for their candidate if they guarantee their vote for Asa. Of course they've probably all promised their votes to Petey Loadsafun, but maybe if you put it to them right you can do business. I'll get some of the boys to help you. You fellows check in here and see me from time to time during the campaign."

"O.K., Rudy," said Shylock.

"We'll see you," said Roger.

"What must I do?" said I.

"Oh, Jesus, I almost forgot," Rudy exclaimed. "Keep him hidden. The less people see him, the better."

"We'll lock him in the chapter room at the house," said Shylock.

"Why can't I go out and campaign?" I asked.

"Shut up," exclaimed Roger.

CHAPTER XVII

Je n'ai pas des cousines, mais j'ai deux tantes.
—GABORIAU

DURING THE DAYS that followed I became quite proficient at Canfield, although I never won a game. After six hundred consecutive losses I cleverly reasoned that something was wrong, and, counting the deck, I found that the five of spades was missing.

I was reasonably happy during my confinement. I had plenty to eat and an oblique view of the sleeping quarters of a sorority house next door. But most of all I liked the mornings, because then I was brought a copy of the Minnesota *Daily* and I could read an account of the election campaign written by Daemon Scoop in his sprightly "new-journalism" style.

Since my sole source of information about the campaign was the Minnesota *Daily,* the best way I can describe it is to list the most pertinent excerpts from the *Daily* news stories:

May 12
Zing! Zang! Zowie!
The lid was blown off the spring elections today as the Yahoo party entered a dark horse in the race for freshman representative to the student council. In a statement issued by his campaign managers, Roger Hailfellow and Shylock Fiscal, the dark horse, Ezra Hearthrug, charged that the Mafia party was "inviting and encouraging" bloodshed and "eventual female extinction."

Hearthrug was referring to a plank in the Mafia party platform stating that male students should remove their

117

hats in elevators when there are women present. "Removing one's hat in an elevator," said Hearthrug, "causes one to take up twice as much room, thereby shrdlu shrdlu shrdlu shrdlu. It is another example of the Mafia party shortsightedness which has always been their chief characteristic."

Hearthrug is a newcomer to campus politics, but, according to his campaign managers, he is amply qualified by virtue of his experience at Salmon P. Chase high school in Whistlestop, Minnesota, his home town, where he served two terms as bursar of the debating society and "made many friends."

May 13

Biff! Bang! Bong!

Etaoin Shrdlu, Mafia candidate for freshman representative to the student council, hurled the charges of Asa (erroneously called Ezra in yesterday's story) Hearthrug, his opponent, back in his (Hearthrug's) teeth today.

"Hearthrug has never heard of chivalry," he said.

"Or if he has," he added, his eyes twinkling slyly, "he probably thinks it is the name of a low-priced car."

May 14

Ricky! Ticky! Tavvy!

Fur flew faster in the spring election today as Asa Hearthrug answered the charges of his opponent, Petey Loadsafun (erroneously called Etaoin Shrdlu in yesterday's shrdlu).

"It is just like the Mafia party," averred Hearthrug, "to dodge a serious issue with a coarse gest. If the Mafia definition of chivalry is to leave broken women in elevators all over Minneapolis, then I'm glad I don't know what it means."

Hearthrug's answer was issued in a prepared statement through his campaign managers, Roger Hailfellow and Shylock Fiscal.

May 15

(Note: This story has nothing to do with the campaign. It is so interesting, however, that I feel I must pass it on.)

An interesting occurrence occurred in Professor Ralph

(Bubbles) Learned's English literature class yesterday.

Three students who have sat next to each other in the class for three semesters discovered that their names are all Alvin Turnverein. They all come from St. Cloud, Minn., where their fathers, all named Pierre, are all engaged in the upholstery business.

Their mothers, all named Grace, were all Duluth girls, and all are slightly discolored as the results of railroad accidents.

The three Alvin Turnvereins are all five feet, eight inches tall, and all speak with pronounced lisps.

They are not related in any way and show a marked dislike for each other.

May 19

Crash! Crunch! Crotch!

Fireworks exploded again today in the race for freshman representative to the student council. Petey Loadsafun, the shrdlu candidate, told your reporter, "I cannot bring myself to worry about the wild accusations of this Hearthrug person. Who is Hearthrug, anyhow? Who ever heard of him?"

May 20

Zis! Boom! Bah!

Still another bombshell was thrown into the spring elections today as Asa Hearthrug answered yesterday's statement of his opponent, Petey Loadsafun.

In a statement issued by his campaign managers, Roger Hailfellow and Shylock Fiscal, Hearthrug said, "Of course nobody has heard of me. I'm a dark horse."

Hearthrug's campaign managers pointed out that Franklin Pierce, too, was a dark horse. Your reporter was unable to ascertain the identity of Franklin Shrdlu.

May 24

(An editorial)

Tomorrow is election day. Another exciting campaign has drawn to a close, and tomorrow, in the good old American tradition, the students will go to the polls and make their choice.

Yet tomorrow is more than election day. It is a demonstration of what a university means in the American scheme of things. It is democracy in action, for a university is something more than an institution of learning; it is a proving ground of democracy.

Consider the newspaper you are reading. It is an example of a fundamental right —freedom of the press. The editor of this newspaper may print what he likes—within certain limits, of course, for freedom is not license. Naturally what appears in this paper must be governed by the considered judgment of the Regents of the University, that august body of men democratically appointed by our duly-elected governor and neglecting their grain and feed stores to devote their talents to the administration of this institution of higher learning.

Similarly, the election tomorrow is an instance of democracy in action. Tomorrow you will be exercising your democratic prerogative. But it is more than a right; it is an obligation too. You may lose it if you do not use it.

So tomorrow get out and vote. The *Daily* makes no recommendations. Although we have followed this extraordinarily lively campaign with acute interest, we feel that we must not tell you *how* to vote. We only tell you *to* vote.

So, no matter who you like, get out there tomorrow and shrdlu.

May 26

Ahhhhhh!

That is the sigh of your reporter. It is a sigh of relief that the hectic election is over, the votes are tabulated, and the winners are chosen.

The magnificent total of 1,382 votes were cast. This figure represents nearly one eleventh of the student body. Coincidentally, it is the exact figure of fraternity and sorority membership on campus.

The winners were . . .

(The rest of this story is illegible. It is blurred with my tears. It tells how bad I lost.)

CHAPTER XVIII

*Docteur, je viens vous demander des nouvelles de
la comtesse.*—RICHELIEU

WELL, I THOUGHT, at least I could lose myself in the
gaiety of the Alpha Cholera spring formal and forget all
about the election. I called Noblesse.

"I mean I'm sorry," she said. "I mean I won't be able
to see you any more. I'm going steady with Petey Loadsafun."

Well, I thought, maybe that's a good thing after all. Now
I won't have to be racking my brains all the time trying
to decide between her and Yetta. And I'll be shut of that
Mother Bloor. I called Yetta.

"Yahoo!" she screamed. "Fascist! Provocateur!"

Neither of them sent back my pins, neither.

CHAPTER XIX

Un cadeau pour moi? Il faut me le montrer.
—BERGSON

IT WAS A BALMY EVENING, typical of the first days of June. The windows of the living room of the Alpha Cholera house were wide open, allowing the fragrance of the outdoors to waft in. Roger and Shylock sat on a low divan talking with Bob Scream, who had come to visit them.

I sat at the desk in the corner of the room with thirty or forty books open in front of me. I was studying for the final examinations that were rapidly approaching. As I plunged into the hard grind of studying, for the first time in weeks I felt a sort of peace. The cold, irrefutable pages of my textbooks blotted out the thoughts of Yetta and Noblesse and the election fiasco that had been making my days hideous. Gratefully I fell into academic forgetfulness.

"You guys want to play a little bridge?" Bob asked.

"Sure," said Roger. "Who can we get for a fourth?"

"Is there anybody upstairs?" Shylock asked.

"No," Roger answered. "They all went down to sorority row to whistle. There's a pretty fair wind up tonight."

"There's Asa sitting over there. Why not ask him?" Bob suggested.

"Let's play three-handed," said Shylock.

"That's no fun," Bob protested. "Let's ask Asa."

"You be his partner?" Roger said.

"No. We'll cut cards. Low man gets him," said Bob.

"And a five-thousand-point handicap," Roger said.

They agreed.

Roger called me. "Asa, come here, old fellow. We're going to play a little bridge."

"No, thanks," I said. "I'm studying for finals."

"Did you hear that, fellows?" asked Roger. "He's studying for finals!"

"Well," said Shylock, "let's not judge him too harshly. Remember, he *is* just a freshman."

"Yes, that's right," said Roger.

"What do you mean?" I asked.

"Well, Asa," said Shylock, "I imagine you want to get through your courses. You don't want to flunk, do you?"

"No," I said simply.

"Well, that's just what you're going to do if you keep on this way. You're going to sit up nights studying. You're going to lose sleep. Your nerves are going to be worn to a fazzle——"

"Frazzle," I interrupted.

"Thank you. Frazzle. By the time you come to take the test you'll be all shot. You'll be lucky if you remember your name, not to speak of the subject matter."

"What must I do?" I asked.

"Relax. That's the only way to prepare for finals. Just relax. Take it from an old hand—it's much more important to be relaxed than to study. You don't see any of us studying, do you?"

"No," I admitted. "But you fellows aren't taking any classes."

"That's not the point," said Shylock. "We never studied."

"Come on and play a little bridge," said Bob. "That's a good way to relax."

"All right," I said.

I should say something here about the way bridge is played on campus. It is a good deal different from the auction I played back home. It is extremely complicated, and I won't pretend that I understood it thoroughly. Every single bid was significant; whatever you said was supposed to tell something to your partner. For instance, here is the first hand we played that night:

Bob held the ace of spades; nine and seven of diamonds,

king, jack, ten, and four of hearts; and ace, queen, seven, six, three, and two of clubs.

Shylock, my partner, held the ace, seven, six, and two of hearts; ten, eight, and four of clubs; king, eight, six, and three of spades; and four and three of diamonds.

Roger held the queen, jack, seven, five, and two of spades; ace, eight, and six of diamonds; eight and three of hearts; and king, jack, and nine of clubs.

I held the queen, nine, and five of hearts; five of clubs; king, queen, jack, five, and two of diamonds; and ten, nine, and four of spades.

Now, then, I had dealt, so I opened the bidding. I said three clubs, indicating that I held the five and two of diamonds and the four of spades.

Bob doubled, indicating that he had the six and seven of clubs.

Shylock kicked me under the table, indicating that he didn't understand my bidding.

Roger passed, indicating that he had the three of hearts.

The bid came back to me. I looked over my hand carefully, and suddenly I discovered something. "Look, kids," I cried laughingly, "I've only got twelve cards."

"Maybe you better go study for finals," said Shylock.

"Finals are very important," said Roger.

"Yes," said Bob. "What you don't get during the course you get in the final."

"You can't be too well prepared," said Shylock.

"All right," I said.

Later I was glad I took their advice, for one must be on one's toes to get good grades at Minnesota. You see, Minnesota is such a large university that it is impossible for the faculty to give individual attention to each student. Instead, students are left to their own devices, and private initiative is stressed. It helps to round out one's personality.

Marks are assigned on the basis of the "curve" or "fang-and-claw" system. Under this system the top 5 per cent of the class gets "A"s and the bottom 5 per cent gets "F"s. In other words, for every student who gets an "A," somebody flunks. The next highest 10 per cent gets "B"s, and the next lowest 10 per cent gets "D"s. The middle 70 per cent gets "C"s.

Much friendly rivalry is engendered by the curve system as students strive for high grades. There are frequently good-natured volleys of gunfire by the "F" students at the "A" students who caused them to be flunked. Often, too, there are interesting contests between students who are trying to beat each other out for top-of-the-class position. I recall an amicable struggle between two girls named Phyllis Mallis and Alice Millis in my Mesopotamian architecture class.

I watched with good-humored interest as Alice spilled ink on Phyllis' lecture notes and Phyllis set fire to Alice's textbooks. Then Alice put scorpions down Phyllis' back and Phyllis squirted acid in Alice's eyes.

So it went, nip and tuck, and as the final examination approached the two friendly rivals were still tied. On the night before the examination Alice stole into Phyllis' room and stealthily pulled all the hair out of her head. She thought that would prevent Phyllis from coming to school and taking the test the next day. But the joke was on Alice. Phyllis got hold of a peruke, came to school the following day, sneaked up behind Alice, who was engrossed in the test, and surreptitiously garroted her with one hundred and twenty feet of sash cord that she had concealed in her tunic.

Some students resort to cheating as they vie for marks under the curve system. I want it understood that I consider this practice entirely reprehensible and that I have never engaged in it myself. Nevertheless, I must admit that I have been impressed by the ingenuity displayed by cheating students.

There are two basic forms of cheating in examinations —the co-operative and the individual. In the co-operative method several students—sometimes the whole class— work together. This method is especially adaptable to examinations of the "True-False" type in which the examiner asks a question that must be answered by writing either "True" or "False." Co-operative cheating in a "True-False" test works this way: a clever, well-informed student sits at the head of the row. If he thinks the answer to a question is "True," he leans his pencil to the left —to the right for "False." The student behind him follows suit, and so on down the line. This gives somewhat the effect of a chorus in a Warner Bros. musical. It is called the "rhythm method."

Individual cheating is even more ingenious. Take the case of Hugh, for example. He made a crib out of one hundred and twenty feet of ticker tape. He took the tape, folded it into accordion pleats, and wrote an answer in each of the folds. The entire abundant source of information fitted snugly in the palm of his hand. Unfortunately, during one test Hugh had trouble finding an answer. He was entangled in seventy feet of tape when one of the proctors, who are always stationed about the room during tests to watch for cheating, suspiciously approached. Luckily at that moment there happened to be a parade going by outside the classroom. Hugh ran to the window, cried "Hurrah," and flung out the ticker tape.

Students with false teeth often tuck folded answer sheets under their dentures and take them out during examinations. Sometimes a proctor comes over and says, "What are you doing?"

"Nothing," they gum innocently.

Less refined cheaters resort to the primitive practice of opening a textbook on the floor beneath their feet. To insure any success for this method the cheater must have an accomplice to blindfold or anesthetize the proctors.

Girls who cheat—and I regret to say there are those who do—use an old but effective method. They insert a crib in the top of their sheer silk stockings and hike up their dirndls for a peek when the going gets tough. I remember a girl named Consuela who did that in one test. She must have been exceedingly uninformed because she kept her skirt up through the whole examination. The proctor saw her all right, but he wasn't going to stop her.

Then, of course, there are the more pedestrian ways of cheating—looking over the shoulder of the one in front of you, talking out of the corner of your mouth to the student beside you, making a crib on your cuff, writing the answers on the classroom wall the day before the test and sitting next to the wall on the day of the test, and bringing a loaf of French bread to class with the answers written on it in poppy seeds.

Needless to say I took my finals honestly, relying solely on what I had learned. The results of the tests were mailed to me several weeks later. I was not to know until the middle of July that I had flunked everything.

CHAPTER XX

Le potage est très chaud.—DALADIER

"GRADUATING SENIORS, members of the faculty, guests, ladies and gentlemen," said the speaker at the commencement exercises which I attended before I went home for the summer, "as I look out over your faces I am reminded of a story. It seems that three Hawaiians went into a music store. 'What can I do for you, gentlemen?' asked the proprietor.

" 'I want a ukulele,' said the first.

" 'And what are you going to do with a ukulele?' asked the proprietor.

" 'I'm going to serenade my girl,' answered the first.

" 'I see,' said the proprietor. He turned to the second. 'What do you want?' he said.

" 'I want a guitar,' said the second.

" 'And what are you going to do with a guitar?'

" 'I'm going to serenade my girl.'

" 'I see,' said the proprietor. He turned to the third. 'What do you want?'

" 'I want a bass drum,' said the third.

" 'And what are you going to do with a bass drum?" asked the proprietor.

" 'Well,' he answered, 'I—— I—— I——'

"Can you beat that? I've forgotten what he said. That'll teach me to make notes. Oh, well, it wasn't really very appropriate anyway. Let's get on with it.

"This night is a happy occasion, happy but at the same time solemn, know what I mean? It is happy because you who are graduating tonight have completed a long and difficult job. It is solemn because now you get to take your places in the world.

"You have a special obligation to the world because you are, like we say, the cream of society. The world is looking to you for leadership. You are going out in the world and make your marks, some of you in business, some in law, some in medicine, some in engineering, some in the arts, and some in business. But all of you are facing the future with the confidence of youth and the comforting knowledge that you are prepared.

"For the Unversity has tried to prepare you. Here the people of the state of Minnesota have provided you with the facilities to partake of the wisdom of the ages. Here, under the good old American horse-sense guidance of the Board of Regents, you have been able to take advantage of one of the finest courses of studies in the country. Here, in addition to your formal education, you have learned something of life—how to make friends, how to deport yourselves, and what decocracy really means.

"The University has been for the last few years your alma mater, your adopted mother. But I wonder how much you really know about the University. You have been so busy with your studies and your activities that you probably have not found time to familiarize yourselves with the glorious history and traditions of the University. I think it fitting then that I should use your last hours here to tell you something of the background of the University.

"The University was founded in 1855. That much is certain. Who founded it is a matter for conjecture. One version has it that the University was founded by an Atlanta textbook salesman named Rhett Fink. It seems that Fink had exhausted the market of Southern colleges, and he was in financial straits. A friend is supposed to have asked him where he intended to sell books now. According to the story, Fink replied, 'I guess I'll have to start a college up North.'

"A brief examination shows that this explanation is apocryphal. In 1855 Fink could not have said, 'I guess I'll have to start a college up North,' because there was no North at that time. North did not come into being until 1908.

"In the spring of 1908 a crazed ptarmigan swooped down on a Long Island estate and carried off in its bill an infant named John Ringling North. The child's father, Cedric (Freckles) North, was frantic with grief. He offered a reward of one million dollars for the return of the boy.

"Everybody on the Atlantic seaboard went out to hunt for the baby. It became a quip of the day to say when someone asked where you were going, 'After North.'

"Later this was shortened to simply 'North,' and that is how the direction got its name.

Another theory about the founding of the University is concerned with Dred Scott. In 1855 Dred Scott came to Minnesota. He took a house in the bend of the Mississippi River where the University now stands and proceeded to write his immortal *Ivanhoe*. One night Scott became involved in a fracas in a Minneapolis rib joint. A quadroon named Joe Riposte was stabbed to death, and Scott was accused of the murder. He was given a summary trial, during the course of which he made his famous 'J'accuse' speech. The jury was unmoved, however, and sentenced him to be hanged.

"Legend has it that after his execution the ghost of Dred Scott returned to haunt the house on the riverbank. On moonless nights it is supposed to have lurked outside the house dismally howling, 'J'accuse.'

"Now, it seems that a St. Paul launderer named Jack Hughes had moved into Scott's house after his (Scott's) execution. One night when Jack Hughes heard the ghost howling 'J'accuse' he thought someone was calling him. He went out to see who it was. In the dark he slipped and fell into the river where he got caught in a strong undertow and drowned.

"Shortly thereafter an itinerant Boston educator named Cotton Mouth drifted by. He saw that the house was vacant and started a little school. That little school, my friends, later became the University of Minnesota, according to the story.

"However it may have begun, Minnesota found itself with a university. But the legislature, except for one member, was singularly unimpressed. That member was William Jennings Bryan. He introduced a bill for funds for the University into the legislature. The solons were apathetic. Then Bryan made his famous 'Cross of Gold' speech. 'What will it be, gentlemen,' he concluded, 'rum, romanism, or rebellion?'

"The legislature was stirred to action. They not only passed the appropriation, but they also lifted Bryan on their shoulders and carried him around the Statehouse. This, however, was not too difficult because Bryan was only six years old at the time and puny for his age.

"Now began a period of expansion. As the campus grew, enrollment figures advanced steadily. More and more farmers, in town for the State Fair, mistook the campus for the fairgrounds, and were seized and pledged into fraternities as they wandered about.

"But physically the campus was still small. Then in 1908 a curious chain of circumstances increased the size of the campus to its present spacious dimensions. Before 1908 the land adjoining the campus belonged to a family called the Chalmers. Perhaps I should not say 'family'; they were more a nation than a family. They were all related. They had an unbreakable custom which allowed only first cousins to marry. Moreover, a woman who was neither pregnant nor nursing was considered something of a pariah.

"You can imagine what their settlement looked like. It was probably the most densely populated place on the whole earth. Every inch of space was occupied by Chalmers—drooling, examining their fingers, snarling over bones, or just staring dully at the ground.

"Curiously enough they had a sort of democracy. One day a year was set aside for elections. On election day they held a monster demonstration. After the monsters were demonstrated the candidates for office made their speeches. Then the elections were conducted.

"But the man who got the *least* number of votes was awarded the office. The theory was that the man who polled the smallest number of votes had the fewest friends, was obligated to the least number of people, and would conduct the least corrupt administration. The funny thing is that the system functioned excellently. The Chalmers enjoyed good government, replete with tax reductions and river and harbor improvement.

"The Chalmers' religion was of the most primitive. From somewhere they had acquired a huge hollow brass statue of Franklin Pierce, an obscure political figure of the last century, I believe. This statue they called Mechel-Dundik and worshiped assiduously. Each evening at nightfall they gathered in front of the statue and stared at it reverently for thirty-five minutes.

"One day in 1908—it was about dusk—two children were playing in front of the statue. They were a brother and sister named Benny and Consuela Chalmers. Benny, who was an adventurous lad for a Chalmers, discovered a crack in the idol and crept inside. His sister was horrified. 'Benny,' she cried, 'you come right out of there.'

" 'No,' said Benny.

" 'You come right out of there,' she repeated, 'or I'll tell Ma.'

" 'Aw, go jump in the lake,' said Benny.

"Meanwhile, the Chalmers had gathered in front of the statue for their evening worship. They heard Benny's command to jump in the lake come out as if from the mouth of Mechel-Dundik. Without a word the whole Chalmers tribe marched off to Lake Calhoun, a short distance away, and jumped in. Unable to swim, they all drowned.

"Benny came out of the idol and found nobody around. He wandered about absently for several days and was finally dispatched by an excitable moccasin snake.

"The land, now ownerless and uninhabited, was given to the University.

"And that, my friends, is a brief background of the glorious institution from which you are graduating tonight. Those are the traditions that lie behind you as you go out into the world to make your marks, some of you in business, some in law, some in medicine, some in engineering, some in the arts, and some in business.

"You must always bear in mind that because you are University graduates you are the leaders of your communities. It is a responsibility, I will not deny. You will soon learn what it is to have people constantly looking up to you. You will say, 'I would like to trade places with

Bill Jones, the welder, or with John Smith, the plumber.' But you really would not. No matter how much more money they make than you, you have advantages that they will never realize.

"For a university is more than just a school. It is a molder of men. And it is more than just a molder of men. It is a molder of ideas. And it is more than just a molder of ideas. It teaches its students not only to think, but to think alike. I am proud to say that wherever you go in this country you find college students holding identical opinions. Often, as a matter of fact, they express them in the same words.

"And when you leave here tonight to go out and make your marks I know that you will not forget your adopted mother any more than you would forget your real mothers. I know that the memory of the University will always remain fresh in your hearts. And I feel sure that all of you, each and every one of you, will join the alumni association and pay your dues promptly. I am positive, too, that each and every one of you will find time to return to the campus occasionally and participate in our reasonably priced reunions. I am certain that you will join wholeheartedly in our new alumni project to subsidize high-school football players in United States territorial possessions like the Hawaiian Islands and Cuba—a vertible gold mine of material, my friends, and completely untouched.

"But it is getting late, and I know you would like to get through here so you can spend this solemn evening among your loved ones. I'll conclude now, and you can get your diplomas.

"Just a word about the diplomas. You get small paper diplomas here tonight, but for another ten dollars you can turn these diplomas in for large, genuine sheepskin reproductions. Naturally, you want a real, long-lasting sheepskin. After all these long and difficult years of going to school you want something more permanent than paper to show for it.

"And in addition to being a thing of beauty, a sheepskin diploma can come in mighty handy sometime. Let me tell you about Mary Ellen N., a girl who graduated from the University a few years ago.

"She graduated in winter. After the commencement exercises a party of her classmates invited her to come on a toboggan party. She tucked her sheepskin diploma in her tunic and accompanied them. It was a dark night and a perilous toboggan slide. The toboggan turned over, and Mary Ellen slid down 1,500 feet of rocky crag. She lost a lot of skin.

"Fortunately, there was a doctor in the party. He saw that quick action was imperative. Quickly he grafted Mary Ellen's diploma on to her skinned member. He saved her life.

"Today Mary Ellen is married to an upholsterer of Rye, New York. She has two lovely children and is prominent in Rye society. Her life is full and perfectly normal except that every time she sits down, she bleats.

"Thank you."

CHAPTER XXI

Il n'y a que deux livres sur la table.—JEANNE D'ARC

THE ENGINEER courteously slowed down to sixty miles an hour to allow me to get off at Whistlestop. Lovable old Father was waiting for me on the platform. "Father!" I cried, and ran to him, tripping in my excitement over Seth Inertia who had been lying since 1905 on the station platform living precariously off of dropped coins.

"My boy," said Father. We embraced in a manly manner. "But you must tell me about yourself. I haven't heard from you in almost a year," he said as we started to walk home.

"You haven't?" I said in amazement. "I wrote you every day."

"Yes, but you see we don't get mail delivered to our house any more," Father explained.

"Why not?"

"Well, the postman, Bert Epistle, won't come to our house ever since your sister Morningstar broke off their engagement."

"Bert? Morningstar? What's all this? When I left home Morningstar was keeping company with a railroad man."

"Yes. That was Tom Trestle. He threw Morningstar over in favor of a lady banjoist who captivated him playing 'Alabama Bound.' Then Morningstar took up with Bert. They got engaged, and it looked like your sister was going to settle down at last."

"Then what happened?"

"Well, one morning a Realsilk man came to the house and asked Morningstar did she want any stockings. She said she didn't rightly know. He said he would try a few pair on her and she could see if she liked them. Well, sir, that fellow was all day putting stockings on Morningstar and taking them off. About nightfall they went away together, and that's the last we ever heard of them."

"I see," I said. "Well, how's Mother? She's still around, I trust."

"It's a funny thing, son," Father answered. "She's disappeared too."

"My God! How did that happen?"

"Strangest think you ever heard of," said Father. "I better start at the beginning. It seems that an Englishman, one Neville O.T.W. (for Oliver Toliver Woliver) Cheyne-Stokes took a trip to Quebec to visit his brother, one Albermarle (Alby) Cheyne-Stokes, a sheep-dip actuary of Montreal. After spending a few weeks in Montreal, Neville Cheyne-Stokes expressed a desire to visit the United States, of which he had heard considerable back home in England. Alby Cheyne-Stokes said that it was a capital idea and that the nicest way to go was by boat across Lake Superior. So bright and early one morning they boarded a Lake Superior excursion boat for the United States.

"It happened that the captain of the boat, a chap named Harris or Benuti, complained of feeling poorly before they embarked. He thought it would be wiser to postpone the trip until he felt better. But the passengers jollied him out of it, saying that he would feel like a new man once he got out on the water and felt the fresh breeze in his face.

"The captain, however, did not feel better. As a matter of fact, he dropped dead about twenty miles out. The boat was left without a pilot. The passengers began to get panicky as they saw the boat tossed this way and that. 'Can anybody here steer a ship?' someone asked.

"The Cheyne-Stokes brothers were below playing Authors at this time, and they did not hear the question clearly. Alby thought someone had asked whether anybody could *ship a steer*. 'I can,' he called, for he had had considerable experience shipping steers as a cattle dealer in Winnipeg in 1923-25.

"When he was led to the pilothouse and told to take over, he was aghast, for he knew nothing whatever about navigation. But looking over the terror-stricken faces of the passengers, he decided that he had better bluff it out. He proceeded to steer the ship.

"Within five minutes he had ripped off the bottom on one of the many coral reefs that abound in Lake Superior. The ship went down with all hands except Neville Cheyne-Stokes who, fearing sea voyages, had concealed an inflated inner tube in his tunic.

"For twenty-nine days and twenty-nine nights Cheyne-Stokes floated on Lake Superior. All he had to eat was a lone guppy that he deftly trapped while the guppy was playing beneath his (Cheyne-Stokes') armpit. Baked all day by the merciless sun, drenched at night by the sudden tropical rain, dismally lonely in the vast wastes of water, Cheyne-Stokes was quite mad when he was finally washed ashore by a capricious tide.

"He thought he was the Earl of Bothwell, that he had landed in Scotland, and that he must find Mary, Queen of Scots. After wandering several days Fate led him to the door of our house.

"It happened that when Cheyne-Stokes came into the house your mother was all dressed and waiting for the new county agricultural agent, one Horst Wessel, to pick her up and take her to the home-canning exhibit in the county seat.

" 'You Mr. Wessel?' she said to Cheyne-Stokes.

"He fell to his knees. 'Ah, true queen,' he cried, 'indeed I am your vassal. Only command me. What will you?'

" 'Looks like a real nice feller,' said your mother.

" 'Come with me, true queen,' he said, 'and I swear'—he swore a terrible oath—'that all shall bow before thy splendor and proclaim thee their true queen. Excelsior!"

"Away they went, and that's the last I ever saw of either of them," Father concluded.

"Then you've been living all alone?" I asked.

"Yes," said Father. "Until yesterday. I hired myself a housekeeper. Damn fine woman. Maybe you know her. She's been working on the campus. Her name is Bloor,"

CHAPTER XXII

Ce stylo-là est celui dont je me sers.—POINCARÉ

AS I MADE MY WAY to the grassy knoll where I knew Lodestone would be waiting I could not help wondering how it would seem when I saw her again. I knew that she would be the same. How would I feel toward her? For I had changed vastly, significantly. Would the simple charms of Lodestone appeal to me, or had my year of amassing knowledge, of rounding out my personality, placed me irrevocably beyond Lodestone? Could the new, sophisticated I be happy with Lodestone—elemental, untutored Lodestone?

Then I saw her. I could not speak. I raised my hand. She saw, and, rising, ran to me, cutting huge irregular furrows in the greensward.

She was in my arms. Our lips touched, pressed, clung. I knew again her yielding, embracing self. Together, as one, we were transported into the searing, timeless ecstasy of us. Now. Now. Now. Now. Now. *Now!*

Peace.

"I been waiting a long time for you," she said.

"Yes, Lodestone," I breathed.

"And I'm hungry," she said.

Nothing had changed.

HE: Hey, Mabel, have you read Max Shulman's latest? It's high-larious! Don't miss RALLY ROUND THE FLAG, BOYS!

SHE: Well, Roger, if you want to read my copy of Max Shulman's wildest —BAREFOOT BOY WITH CHEEK —bring up your copy of "RALLY" and we'll trade.

HE: Be right over!

FIFTY BESTSELLERS AT 50c EACH

Whatever your preference, you'll find hours of reading pleasure from the books in this listing.

- ☐ F1749 **COWHAND: THE STORY OF A WORKING COWBOY**, Fred Gipson
  The West is not dead! This is a book about the way the West is now.
- ☐ F1735 **CRIME AND PUNISHMENT**, Fyodor Dostoevsky
  Unchallenged as the most searching exploration of the guilty mind.
- ☐ F1703 **FANCIES AND GOODNIGHTS**, John Collier
  50 superb stories of the weird and fantastic.
- ☐ F1688 **ART OF MIXING DRINKS**, The Esquire Drink Book
  Sophisticated—Entertaining—Lively! Everything you need to know.
- ☐ F1687 **DODGE CITY: QUEEN OF COWTOWNS**, Stanley Vestal
  For 14 years it was the wickedest little city in the U. S. A.
- ☐ F1675 **H. M. PULHAM, ESQ.**, John P. Marquand
  The story of a rich, proper Bostonian who fell in love with a girl who didn't belong.
- ☐ F1665 **PARENTS' GUIDE TO CHILDREN'S ILLNESSES**, Dr. John Henderson
  Practical, authoritative guide to the illnesses of children.
- ☐ F1662 **OLD SANTA FE TRAIL**, Stanley Vestal
  Story of the richest, wildest trail in all of North America.
- ☐ F1661 **INDIAN FIGHTING ARMY**, Fairfax Downey
  The army that faced the toughest, smartest, cruelest foemen of all.
- ☐ F1649 **NEW CAMPUS WRITING II**, Nolan Miller (ed.)
  The best work by today's most exciting new authors.
- ☐ F1648 **DRUMS ALONG THE MOHAWK**, Walter D. Edmonds
  The fierce and bloody days when the pioners held the frontier against the British.
- ☐ F1622 **EYELESS IN GAZA**, Aldous Huxley
  A brilliant amoral man's search for meaning in a life without standards.
- ☐ F1620 **ONLY YESTERDAY**, Frederick Lewis Allen
  American manners, morals and politics in the amazing decade, the glittering 20's.
- ☐ F1616 **AMY VANDERBILT'S EVERYDAY ETIQUETTE**
  Hundreds of answers to our everyday etiquette questions.
- ☐ F1597 **LORD JIM**, Joseph Conrad
  Immortal story of man's guilt, his pursuit of the truth and his final redemption.
- ☐ F1572 **CASS TIMBERLANE**, Sinclair Lewis
  Great story of a mature man who marries a passionate young girl half his age.
- ☐ F1556 **NEW SOUTHERN HARVEST**, Robert Penn Warren (ed.)
  Short stories by contemporary Southern writers.
- ☐ F1537 **SHANNON'S WAY**, A. J. Cronin
  A dedicated medical scientist who learned he had to master his own temptations.
- ☐ F1510 **WATERFRONT**, Budd Schulberg
  The whole gripping story the movie couldn't tell.
- ☐ F1495 **APACHE LAND**, Ross Santee
  An unforgettable look into the last wild fastness of the old West and its memorable men.
- ☐ F1494 **LOST PONY TRACKS**, Ross Santee
  The Arizona range in the days when cowboys were still cowboys.
- ☐ F1474 **KEYS OF THE KINGDOM**, A. J. Cronin
  A magnificent story of the great adventure of goodness.
- ☐ F1454 **POINT OF NO RETURN**, John P. Marquand
  A man imprisoned in the grip of circumstances beyond his control.
- ☐ F1445 **LIFE ON THE MISSISSIPPI**, Mark Twain
  Worth reading again and again. A vivid recalling of the gusty American past.
- ☐ F1442 **INSPIRATIONAL READER**, William Oliver Stevens (ed.)
  Over 500 selections from the Holy Bible. A key to hope, courage and strength.
- ☐ F1441 **GOLDEN ARGOSY**, Van H. Cartmell & Chas. Grayson (ed.)
  Richly laden treasury of the most often read short stories in the English language.
- ☐ F1429 **CITADEL**, A. J. Cronin
  Humanity's endeavor to conquer disease and death!
- ☐ F1428 **DAY LINCOLN WAS SHOT**, Jim Bishop
  Hour by hour story of the greatest crime in American History.

BANTAM BOOKS, INC., Dept. A, 657 W. Chicago Ave., Chicago 10, Illinois
Please send me the Bantam Bestsellers which I have checked.

Name......................................

Address...................................

City......................................

State.....................................

I am enclosing $..................
(Check or Money Order — NO CURRENCY PLEASE.)
SORRY, no C.O.D.'s

NOTE: Please include 10¢ per book for postage and handling on orders of less than 5 books.

ALLOW TWO TO THREE WEEKS FOR DELIVERY